Paris Connection

A Paradox Murder Mystery

Book Five

Charles J Thayer

Paris Connection

This story is a work of fiction.

Cover

Shutterstock: Samot

Paris Connection

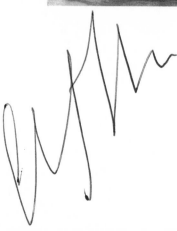

Dedication

Global Coronavirus Pandemic

This book is dedicated to all the essential service workers who risk their health by going to work every day.

Health care professionals, law enforcement officers, grocery store clerks, drug store staff, mail carriers, truck drivers, delivery personnel, teachers, bank tellers and all the others who are out there every day doing their jobs.

The media is right, you are heroes!

Stay Safe

Prologue

My name is Steve Wilson. Four years ago, I was Chief Auditor at one of our nation's largest banks headquartered in New York City. After thirty-five years of corporate life, I elected to take early retirement at age fifty-five.

I've always enjoyed the challenge of solving financial crimes. After my retirement, I founded Paradox-Research to investigate fraud and money laundering. I didn't expect to solve murders.

Today's technology gives me the flexibility to work, write and travel aboard Paradox, my custom-designed Maine-built lobster boat. I enjoy sharing the results of my investigations with you as works of fiction.

Welcome aboard,

Steve

Aboard Paradox
Paradox09A@Gmail.com

1

Late January - Palm Beach, Florida

"Damn - Look at this email from Mark!"

Steve,

I just learned Margot Dubois was found dead in her Paris apartment. She was in New York helping our office with an investigation this week and returned to Paris on the red-eye Thursday night. Pierre Rochat, the French bank's attorney, called me this morning. He said Margot's femme de ménage discovered her body late Friday morning and a medical exam is being performed.

I will let you know more as events unfold. Sorry to share such tragic news.

Mark Bouchard

Amanda's puzzled, "Who's Margot?"

"She worked for me in Paris as Senior Auditor for our banking operations in Europe. Margot was smart, ambitious, worked long hours, and earned this important management position in her early thirties. She was my representative with Mark's team on a foreign money laundering case two years before I retired."

I continue, "Everyone she encountered at the bank admired her. She was a remarkable young woman with a bright future. Margot was very talented, and a large French bank recruited her to be their Chief Auditor three years ago."

"I'm sorry. What do you think happened?"

"This is very strange. I need to learn more and arrange a meeting with Mark in New York next week."

#   #   #

Amanda and I are spending the weekend aboard Paradox, my custom Maine-built lobster boat. We both relish a break from winter weather, and she escaped a snowstorm in Maine to join me Friday evening for our late January break at Palm Harbor Marina in Palm Beach.

We crossed paths when Amanda was investigating a murder four years ago during my first post-retirement visit to Maine. Today, she is a Special FBI Agent investigating suspicious financial activities. Our romantic relationship developed two years ago when she was assigned to help me investigate a suspected Ponzi scheme.

Amanda lives in Maine, and I enjoy working from my boat in Florida during the winter. We try to overcome fifteen-hundred miles of separation with occasional weekend rendezvous and frequent phone calls.

Sunday evening, Amanda places her small leather backpack and canvas duffel bag in the taxi taking her to the airport for her return flight to Portland.

She has a meeting at the FBI's New York office the following week, and we plan to spend next weekend together in New York.

I return to my co-op apartment in New York on Tuesday with plans to meet Mark at his office on Thursday morning.

Wednesday, Mark sends a follow-up email:

Steve,

The Paris bank's Chief Legal Officer, Pierre Rochat, said Margot's medical report indicates she died shortly after she returned to her apartment Friday morning. The exam detected sleeping medication in her system, but it was below a lethal level. The police found no sign of forced entry, theft, physical harm, or sexual assault. The medical examiner ruled her cause of death to be from natural causes.

Margot's body has been released and her family plans to have her service in Moneteau, her hometown.

Mark Bouchard

2

New York City

Mark Bouchard is Director of the FBI's Financial Crimes Division. We developed a strong professional relationship during my banking career when we spent untold hours working on cases together in his New York office. Following my retirement, we established an occasional consulting relationship between the FBI's Financial Crimes Division and my firm, Paradox-Research.

I ignore the freezing wind on my face as I step over dirty slush and walk to Mark's mid-town office a few blocks from my apartment. I sign in with lobby security and see Mark waiting for me as I exit the elevator. A somber expression replaces his usual smile as we stop at the coffee machine before walking to his office.

Mark invites me to his sofa, "Sorry to report such sad news. Margot was a rare blend of charm and talent. It was a delight to work with her."

I agree, "I was very proud of her. Thanks for your emails and for finding time to meet me today. Have you learned anything new?"

Mark continues, "No, Margot's death was a shock. She was in New York helping my team investigate a complex money laundering case last week. I'm thankful she stopped by my office for a visit before she returned to Paris."

Mark frowns, "Pierre said the medical examiner didn't identify any physical trauma or illegal drugs in her system and he determined Margot died of natural causes. She was physically fit and appeared to be in good health. I'm puzzled by the results of her medical exam."

"I agree, it's hard to believe she just died in her sleep at age thirty-seven. What do you think?"

"You taught her well, and Margot had great instincts for detecting fraud. She recently identified foreign accounts in France being used to fund illegal political activities in our country. That's why she was in New York. As you've experienced, it's easy to make enemies when investigating the activities of hostile foreign governments."

I reflect, "True. Before I retired, Margot and I were investigating a foreign money laundering case with your office. The personal threats she and Sarah received were not subtle. That's when Margot and I both moved to more secure buildings and you placed Sarah in the witness protection program."

I pause, "Have you contacted Sarah?"

"No, it was your investigation and Margot worked for you. I thought you would want to share the sad news with Sarah."

"They became friends during our investigation and were disappointed when you said, for Sarah's safety, they should avoid future contact."

I ask, "Do you think Margot's death is connected to one of her investigations?"

"No reason to think so. However, her unexpected death and the inconclusive medical exam make me uncomfortable. Do you plan to attend her service?"

I answer, "Yes, I contacted Pierre and booked a flight to Paris. He will drive me to Moneteau."

"Maybe you can learn more. Margot developed her curious nature working for you."

#   #   #

I'm uncomfortable sharing sad news. Mark is Sarah's official witness protection contact, and I wish he had called her. I don't know Sarah's new identity or location, but Mark authorized an encrypted email account at Paradox-Research for us to communicate. I email her and prepare myself for a painful conversation.

Sarah,

Sad news. Margot died in Paris last week, and I plan to attend her service next week. Call me.

Sorry, Steve

Sarah is a fictitious name and she always 'spoofs' her new identity and number when she calls me.

Ten minutes later, my phone flashes 'Picasso' and Sarah asks, "What happened?"

3

February – New York City

It's crisp and cold when I meet Amanda's flight Friday night at LaGuardia Airport. I'm amused when I see young men take a second look at Amanda with her red ski jacket, blue jeans, black leather boots and long blond ponytail as she exits security. I suspect they would be surprised to learn she is an FBI Agent in her mid-forties and carries a Glock 19 in her small black leather backpack. After a warm embrace and envious glances, we walk to the taxi stand.

The slush from last week's winter snow has melted, and the forecast for the first week of February is crisp and sunny. We enjoy touring neighborhood art galleries on Saturday and walk hand-in-hand to attend a jazz performance at Lincoln Center Sunday evening.

It's still dark Monday morning when Amanda brews our coffee and toasts bagels before walking to Mark's office. It's not unusual for her to attend periodic meetings at the New York office, and we avoid sharing confidential details about our assignments.

# # #

Amanda is beaming as she enters my apartment at six o'clock Monday evening. I offer her a glass of Pinot Grigio after she changes from her dark blue pantsuit into her typical jeans and a pale blue sweater.

"OK. You're smiling like a Cheshire Cat. What can you tell me?"

"Mark said we can discuss my new assignment, but I'm not at liberty to discuss our findings."

She takes a deep breath. "Mark selected me to be his representative on a special joint task force with members from the CIA and Treasury Department. Our assignment is to assimilate information from other agents and identify hostile governments sponsoring cyberattacks."

"An increasing number of attacks utilize fake emails to plant ransomware on computers to block access to all data. The perpetrators then demand ransom paid in bitcoin to unlock computer data. The amounts are affordable in most cases, and many organizations just pay. However, the growing volume of reported attacks is generating millions of dollars each month for the perpetrators."

"Hackers based offshore are responsible for most of these attacks. Talented programmers can disguise their location and steal information from around the world. A few years ago, these attacks were by freelancers using fake emails to steal personal information. Today's attacks are more sophisticated and target individuals, corporations, and governments. Mark will present our classified report to a Congressional Committee in May."

"I start next Monday and we will work in New York. Mark wants me to attend the hearing in Washington with him. I need to return to Portland tomorrow morning to transfer my current investigations to agents in Boston. I also need to buy outfits for working in New York since my sweaters and jeans are not appropriate for this office."

She pauses, "Mark authorized a hotel for me when I return next week, but I told him I prefer to stay with you. My assignment requires a new security clearance so, if I'm invited, you will also be subject to a new background check."

I chuckle, "Invitation extended."

"Accepted", with a soft kiss.

I'm grinning like a kid opening a birthday gift, "A toast to your new assignment, well done!"

"This is exciting. Your new assignment will let us spend more time together in New York. I can work from my apartment and non-stop flights make it convenient for us to go to Palm Beach and enjoy more warm weekends together on Paradox."

4

Paris, France

Amanda leaves the apartment at daybreak Tuesday morning to take her flight to Portland. Margot's service is this week, and my flight for Paris departs Tuesday night.

My red-eye flight lands at Paris Orly Airport early Wednesday morning. Fortunately, I can sleep on overnight flights to Europe and am alert when a taxi takes me past the Eiffel Tower, across the Seine, and around the Arc de Triomphe to a small hotel in the 8th arrondissement of Paris.

I have time to unpack, shower, and change from my jeans into a dark blue pinstripe suit. It's only a short walk to the bank's headquarters, and I meet Pierre at nine o'clock to join him for the two-hour drive to Moneteau, a small town near Auxerre in the wine region best known for Chablis.

Hollywood could cast Pierre as a bank attorney in a classic French movie. We both have salt and pepper hair but his trim mustache accents his stocky build. His solid blue double-breasted suit, blue bowtie, pocket handkerchief, and matching double-breasted overcoat are a sharp contrast to my more traditional single-breasted attire. He stands six inches below my height of six-feet and looks to weigh twenty pounds less than my two-hundred pounds. He reminds me of Agatha Christie's fictional detective, Hercule Poirot.

"Monsieur Wilson, thank you for coming to Margot's service. I have spoken with her mother and the family is grateful you are attending. Margot always gave you credit for helping her career. Her mother says Margot admired you and shared her respect for you with her family."

"Please call me Steve. Thank you for making the hotel arrangements. I consider Margot a friend and appreciate the opportunity to visit with you on our drive to Moneteau."

"You may address me as Pierre, but I prefer Monsieur Rochat with bank employees. The bank's garage attendant has my car waiting, and I welcome your company on our drive."

We exit the elevator into the garage lobby and the attendant rushes to open the doors of a gleaming black Porsche Panamera.

Pierre says, "You had an impressive banking career and I'm surprised you elected to take early retirement. I enjoy the prestige and can't imagine not working for the bank. However, your new firm is now a recognized authority on bank fraud. I'm curious, why Paradox?"

"A paradox is a self-contradictory proposition that when investigated may prove to be true. For example, '*This statement is false*' is a paradox, if true then the statement cannot be false. Many financial crimes are structured as a paradox to confuse investigators."

Pierre furrows his brow. "I see your point, and why is 09A added to your email address?"

"09A is the crime code for murder."

"Humm………..Is that because you write murder mysteries in your spare time?"

"My novels are based on my investigations. My next book, *Synthetic Escape*, will be published shortly."

Pierre is pensive, "I seldom have time to read for pleasure, but must buy it."

I ask, "The bank's website shows you were elected Chief Legal Counsel ten years ago. What did you do before you joined the bank?"

Pierre smiles, "I was born and attended school in Switzerland. I moved to Paris for law school and worked at a Paris law firm for fifteen years before joining the bank as Chief Legal Counsel. The bank was one of my clients at the law firm, so the transition was easy. I serve as Secretary to our board and my duties have expanded over the years to include management of our administrative services. I'm Secretary to the audit committee and worked closely with Margot."

The cold and cloudy morning adds to the dreary atmosphere and our uncomfortable silence as we continue our two-hour drive to Moneteau. I finally ask, "Can you tell me more about what happened?"

Pierre sighs, "The police discussed the results of their investigation with me and they reported nothing suspicious. Margot arrived home at five o'clock Friday morning from her overnight flight. Her femme de ménage found her lying fully dressed on her bed. The police found no sign of forced entry, theft, physical harm, sexual assault, and nothing appeared disturbed. The medical exam found no signs of trauma, so they concluded she died of natural causes."

"Margot's family allowed me to enter her apartment after the police completed their investigation. My assistant and I went to the apartment Monday afternoon. We agreed, nothing appeared disturbed and my assistant collected Margot's belongings. We had a bank courier deliver them to her mother in Moneteau."

Pierre pauses, "However, we have a mystery. I recovered her mobile phone, but Margot's laptop was not inside the stylish leather case she always carried. My assistant and I could not locate her laptop. It's standard bank protocol to freeze all passwords to prevent access to bank files after an employee's death. No attempts have been made to use Margot's passwords to access bank systems."

"Our security systems give us the ability to locate a mobile phone or laptop when activated online, but we've detected no activity."

I'm puzzled, "This is news to me. Who had access to her apartment?"

"To my knowledge, only the police and the femme de ménage. The police had yellow crime scene tape across the doorway, but her apartment was unlocked when we entered Monday afternoon. The building is very secure and requires a keypad code to enter a locked foyer monitored by security cameras. The residents use the security cameras to view visitors and must enter an individual code to admit a guest. The cameras record everyone coming into or leaving the building."

Pierre continues, "Louis, Margot's assistant, is attending the service with the bank's audit team. I've recommended Louis assume her role until the committee selects her successor. The audit function reports directly to Sebastian Hedinger, Chair of our audit committee. As Secretary to the committee, I work closely with our audit function and I'm confident Louis can manage the existing caseload."

He hesitates, "However, Sebastian is not certain Louis has sufficient experience to be Margot's permanent replacement."

"Is there anything I can do to help?"

Pierre looks surprised. "I suppose you could help us evaluate Louis. He will be at the church and I plan for both of us to sit with the bank's audit staff at Margot's service."

5

Moneteau, France

We pass vineyards in the countryside near Moneteau and arrive at a small stone church overflowing with Margot's family and friends. Pierre finds a space to park along the narrow road and we walk together to locate Margot's family inside. I'm not fluent in French, and thankful Pierre provides the introductions.

"Monsieur Wilson, I am Marie, Margot's younger sister. Our parents speak very little English. We are all grateful you came to Moneteau. Margot spoke of you so often that we think of you as family."

"Marie, I never know what to say. Sorry seems so inadequate. Your sister was a very talented person, and I was very proud of her. I wanted to attend to show my respects to Margot and your family."

Marie translates my condolences to her parents, and my limited French suffices to recognize her translation is more eloquent than my own words.

I'm speechless by the heart-felt hug from Margot's mother and feel her warm tears against my cheek as she embraces me.

Margot's father squeezes my hand, but he does not speak. He attempts to hide his emotion, but his ashen face reveals his pain.

Marie whispers, "Please join us. We have a seat in the family section for you."

She takes my hand and I feel awkward as we leave Pierre standing alone to join the bank's audit staff.

After the service, Marie introduces me to Margot's friends and translates my condolences. I'm pleased to see colleagues from our former bank approach her parents with their expressions of sympathy, and I excuse myself for a brief visit with them.

When I return, Pierre is introducing Margot's staff to her parents. I approach Marie as Pierre and the bank's audit staff depart the church.

"Marie, please excuse me, it's time for me to return to Paris. Pierre was kind to drive me, and I must return with him to my hotel. This is my card. Please contact me if there is anything I can do."

Tears are still visible as she replies, "Thank you, we are very grateful you came to Moneteau." I am surprised by her warm embrace.

When I exit, I see Pierre waiting with a small group along the walkway to the church entrance. He speaks as I approach, "Monsieur Wilson, I want to introduce you to Margot's staff."

"Hello, Monsieur Wilson. I am Louis, Margot's assistant. She spoke highly of you and we are pleased you came today. We all miss her."

"Thank you, she was a special person. Many people will miss Margot."

Louis begins introductions and Pierre interrupts, "I have meetings this afternoon, but asked Louis to join us for dinner tonight. It will give you an opportunity to visit before you return to New York tomorrow morning."

Pierre breaks the silence on our return trip to Paris. "Attending a funeral for such a vibrant young woman is exceptionally sad."

I respond, "Yes, very sad. The circumstances seem strange and the missing laptop concerns me. Do you think it's related to her death?"

Pierre hesitates, "I doubt it. Her apartment was unlocked over the weekend, and the police suspect a resident or service staff took it. At my request, the police checked the security cameras."

"Did the cameras show anyone entering the building after Margot arrived home?"

"No. The police told me she entered the building alone shortly after five o'clock and there is no evidence anyone followed her."

Pierre says, "I hope you don't mind, I invited Louis to join us tonight. Dinner will give you an opportunity to learn more about him and I look forward to your opinion."

# # #

I'm pleased Pierre reserved a small suite in a historic hotel for my stay in Paris. I prefer to stay in older hotels with local character as the rooms in modern facilities are identical. The antique French furniture in my suite isn't comfortable, but the new mattress is perfect. I have time for a nap to help me adjust to the six-hour time change. Two hours later, I shave and take a refreshing shower in an elegant marble bathroom. I unpack a fresh white shirt, select a nautical tie, and retrieve my pinstripe suit for our dinner at the hotel.

Louis greets me in the ornate foyer ten minutes before eight o'clock, "Bonsoir, I look forward to dinner tonight. Monsieur Rochat is a busy man and might be late. He frequently runs behind schedule and his secretary asks me to join others waiting outside his office for meetings."

Louis appears surprised when the Maître d'hôtel welcomes Pierre at eight. "Bonsoir Monsieur Pierre, let me help you with your overcoat."

I notice the distinctive label from a custom Savile Row tailor as the Maître d'hôtel hands Pierre's coat to the young woman at the vestiaire.

"We have your private room waiting for you."

A young woman wearing a tuxedo opens the door to a private room with an antique table set for three. She directs us to our seats and opens a bottle of Bordeaux wine for Pierre to taste. Pierre smiles, "Merci, this is superb!"

She pours a glass for each of us and Pierre raises his glass; "Château Lafite Rothschild is a personal favorite. I hope you enjoy it, a votre santé!"

Louis glances in my direction and follows my lead as I lift my glass. "A splendid wine. You have exquisite taste and a glass of Lafite Rothschild is a rare treat for me."

Pierre beams in appreciation of my compliment.

Louis reveals a nervous smile. "An excellent wine. Thank you for inviting me to dinner tonight. I look forward to our visit with Monsieur Wilson."

"Please, call me Steve, and it's my pleasure to dine with you this evening."

Louis continues, "Margot told me you were her most important mentor, and she was very grateful for your guidance. She quoted you frequently and wanted to provide the same guidance for her team. We were very fortunate to work for her."

Pierre is the perfect host and raises his wine glass as an excellent five-course dinner featuring roasted duck is served. "Bon appétit!"

Pierre excuses himself after dinner, "Perhaps you can visit a while longer, but I have an early meeting tomorrow and need my rest."

We all stand and I say, "Thank you for a marvelous evening. Dinner was superb, and the Lafite was a spectacular choice."

Louis is pensive as Pierre walks away. "Monsieur Rochat said he is asking your advice on succession. I hope to be selected as Chief Auditor. What can I do or say to convince you I am ready?"

I motion for us to sit and remove my suit coat. "Let's relax and enjoy the last of the Lafite. I'm not as formal as Pierre."

Louis exhales, "Merci."

I continue, "Pierre told me about Margot's missing laptop. The circumstances of her death and the missing laptop concern me. I volunteered to help when he mentioned succession. Pierre told me you will manage the transfer of her investigations to other members of your team. I'm curious if her laptop is connected to one of those investigations. I can offer you a fresh set of eyes to see if I spot anything suspicious."

Louis's reply is more relaxed. "We are all concerned about her laptop and your thoughts are welcome. How do we arrange your participation?"

"I'm willing to serve as an unpaid volunteer, no need to approve a formal consulting agreement. I can email Pierre and say such an informal arrangement will help me evaluate your experience. We only need to sign the bank's standard confidentiality agreement."

#   #   #

My early morning walk through the historic Paris neighborhood is refreshing and I stop at a small

---

28

café for a breakfast of croissants, fresh fruit, and coffee. Paris is a charming city, even on an overcast winter day. Amanda's assignment will be over by Memorial Day, so we should plan a visit to this romantic city.

I stroll through a nearby park on my return to the hotel to pack and pay my bill. I'm surprised when the desk clerk says, "Monsieur Wilson, you have no charges. Monsieur Pierre arranged for you to stay as a guest of the bank. He has a limousine waiting to drive you to the airport."

#   #   #

My flight lands in New York Thursday afternoon and I call Amanda from the taxi. We have plans to meet for the weekend and I'm eager to learn when she expects to arrive.

She sighs, "My new assignment is more time-consuming than expected. Transferring my current assignments and completing my security clearance will consume all weekend. I won't arrive at the apartment until late Sunday night. Your security interview is Saturday morning."

"That's OK. I can meet the FBI Agent for my interview and then spend the balance of my weekend working on the proof copy of *Synthetic Escape*."

6

Denver, Colorado

It's still dark Monday morning when Amanda brews our coffee and toasts bagels before walking to the office. I don't see her again until nine o'clock at night. My cooking for two is problematic, so we walk to a nearby café for a late dinner.

Once we're seated, she says, "Sorry I'm so late. How was your day?"

"I go to Denver tomorrow night to discuss a new investigation for a brokerage client, but I'm preoccupied with Margot's death."

"You had a fast trip. How was Margot's service?"

"Lots of tears – everyone is in shock. Pierre, the bank's Chief Legal Counsel, made the hotel arrangements and drove me to Moneteau. Margot's family was very appreciative I attended. Marie, Margot's younger sister, acted as my interpreter."

"Pierre hosted a fancy dinner in Paris and I visited with Margot's assistant. Louis wants to be Margot's successor. I volunteered to help Pierre determine if Louis is qualified. I emailed Pierre today and suggested we sign a confidentiality agreement so I can work with Louis."

I hesitate, "Pierre told me Margot's laptop is missing and I'm curious if an investigation has something to do with her death."

Amanda is skeptical, "I thought you said the medical exam concluded she died of natural causes. Why would anyone kill Margot to steal a laptop?"

"The medical examiner found no sign of drugs or physical trauma. However, I'm surprised he didn't identify a specific cause of death. I called Mark today to make certain he knows about her laptop. It contains information about an FBI money laundering case connected to the Paris bank."

#   #   #

I take a taxi to LaGuardia Tuesday afternoon for my flight to Denver. The plane has a rough landing and I experience a thrilling taxi ride on icy roads to my downtown hotel.

It's still windy and snowing when I walk from my hotel to the brokerage firm's downtown office Wednesday morning. Daniela, the brokerage firm's regional manager, greets me and we adjourn to a small conference room with a view of the skyline. Curt, the firm's compliance officer, joins us and he motions to the window. "Sorry about the snow. Hope your flight was on time."

"No delays; the Denver airport is accustomed to winter weather. What can you tell me about your insider trading investigation?"

Daniela says, "Our investigation started when the stock exchange sent us a routine notification about a suspicious transaction in an account."

Curt continues, "We checked the account and discovered a pattern of suspicious trades. A college student named Logan Levy has a remarkable ability to buy stocks before public acquisition announcements. He sells the shares and transfers his gains to a linked money market account at our firm. His withdrawals show his profits are used to pay college expenses. His investments are all under twenty thousand, and his activity slipped under our radar. He owns no stocks today and his money market account has a balance of eighteen thousand dollars."

Daniela adds, "We reported thirteen suspicious transactions to securities regulators and attempted to investigate. Our previous cases of insider trading have been easy to trace and solve. Our last case was stock purchased by a board member's daughter – I can't believe she expected to get away with it."

Curt says, "This student's trading success is a mystery and we can't identify an obvious insider connection. We plan to tell our regulators we have retained you to investigate."

I spend Wednesday afternoon downloading and organizing Logan's account profile and securities transactions on my laptop. The snowstorm has passed and I have dinner with a former banking colleague Wednesday night before returning to New York Thursday morning.

7

Palm Beach – Presidents' Day Weekend

It's raining when I take a taxi from LaGuardia back to my apartment late Thursday afternoon. I'm looking forward to going to sunny Florida and spending the upcoming Presidents' Day weekend with Amanda.

She works late again, so we meet at a neighborhood café for dinner. After a warm hug, she asks about my trip to Denver.

"It will be an intriguing assignment. Somehow, a college student has a remarkable ability to buy stocks prior to acquisition announcements."

I smile and touch her hand, "Let's change the subject. I've had a busy couple of weeks and I'm looking forward to our Presidents' Day weekend."

Amanda frowns, "Sorry, but we need to cancel my flight to Palm Beach tomorrow. This assignment is more complex than I expected, and I need to work over the holiday weekend. You can still go. I know you will enjoy a few warm days in Florida."

I sigh, "I'm disappointed you won't be with me. No question, I'm spoiled working from the boat and prefer Florida's warmer weather this time of year."

Amanda says, "I hope to get a handle on this assignment in the next few weeks so we can start spending more time together. Sorry, this isn't working as we expected."

I give her hand a soft squeeze, "I understand, we'll make it work."

# # #

Friday afternoon, I fly to Palm Beach alone. I miss Amanda and occupy my time with long walks, bike rides, lunch at a café on Clematis, dinner at a French bistro, and working with my laptop on my boat's aft deck.

Palm Harbor Marina

Paradox has a custom interior equipped with a small built-in desk and my onboard technology provides secure WiFi, cellular and satellite communications. I enjoy my new-found sense of freedom and have spent most of my time living and working aboard since retiring from the bank.

The challenge of a new assignment always stimulates me and the holiday weekend gives me an opportunity to start my Denver assignment. I begin by examining acquisition announcements, looking for common links between transactions. My goal is to identify an insider common to all the transactions. Leaks can occur at any level including from board members, investment banks, and law firms negotiating the mergers.

I input the names of every board member, lawyer, law firm, investment bank, and investment banker into a specialized program for analysis. The program searches for a common link between the merger transactions. However, the diagram it creates looks like a spider web. Nothing links a single firm or person to every transaction.

I'm baffled. Thirteen trades made by this young student during the past year have resulted in gains following merger announcements. He has averaged at least one profitable investment every month. He made each of his investments a week or more prior to any published rumor or public announcement of an acquisition.

Two of Logan's investments didn't result in a merger related profit, but my research shows they follow a similar pattern. Published rumors of a transaction occurring after he makes his investment prove to be false. Humm……. every trade is associated with an actual or rumored merger transaction.

My suspicions are not sufficient to obtain a search warrant to examine Logan's electronic records to search for his insider source. His social media accounts show he is a fun-loving student working on his graduate degree in history. I find nothing in Logan's background suggesting any financial knowledge or investment experience.

8

New York City

On Tuesday, I return to New York to be with Amanda. Most of our previous time together has been weekends and vacations aboard Paradox. I'm trying to be sensitive to the changes required for us to live together in my New York apartment.

The classified nature of Amanda's new assignment requires her to work at the FBI office. However, living with me and working in a New York office is dramatically different from being a field agent in Maine. Her use of the closet and bathroom in the spare bedroom I use as my office isn't an issue for me because she's gone before I start my workday.

Amanda's daily presence is easier for me to accommodate as I didn't need to make major changes for her to move into my apartment. My biggest adjustment is spending more than a few days in New York. Since retirement, I've spent most of my time living and working aboard Paradox and seldom use the new desk in my spare bedroom.

Wednesday morning, we snuggle close before she gets out of bed, brews our coffee, and gets dressed for work. It's still dark when we kiss as she leaves the apartment. My morning routine starts with a walk to my old neighborhood gym for a short workout and a stop at a café for breakfast.

The Paris bank's confidentiality agreement arrives by email an hour after I return to my apartment. I immediately sign the agreement and return it by email. Louis calls an hour later with my passcode to access a 'read-only' file on the Paris bank's computer system.

Wednesday afternoon I send a text to Mark:

"Just FYI, I signed a confidentiality agreement with the Paris bank today and they've provided 'read-only' access to Margot's files. I've volunteered to help spot any suspicious activity related to her missing laptop."

My curiosity about Margot's death and her laptop moves a review of her active investigations to the top of my priority list. Paris is six hours ahead of New York, so I schedule a follow-up conference call with Louis for Friday morning at eight o'clock in New York, two o'clock in the afternoon in Paris.

#   #   #

Friday morning, "Louis, help me understand how Margot managed your audit department. How did she manage routine audits, conduct investigations, and present your findings to the audit committee?"

Louis explains, "The committee approves our annual audit plan each December. We establish new audit files with sequential codes at the beginning of each year. For example, the first file this year was 20-101 and we are at 20-134. Our aim is to confirm transactions conform to financial regulations and bank policy. We all do periodic audits of the bank's operations and reported any suspicious activity to Margot."

"She opened new audit files, reviewed our findings, authorized new investigations, and delegated most assignments to a staff member. Margot also conducted audits and investigations. She wanted her staff to be knowledgeable about our entire caseload and she reviewed the status of routine audits and active investigations with us at our Monday morning staff meetings."

"We prepare monthly reports for Monsieur Rochat to send to Monsieur Hedinger with the audit committee minutes and proposed agenda. Margot attended all audit committee meetings, and I accompanied her most of the time. She provided verbal summaries of routine audits, described active investigations, and answered questions. We hold private sessions with the committee members without bank management at the end of each meeting. Monsieur Rochat serves as Secretary for the audit committee and prepares the minutes."

Louis concludes, "I am following the same procedure and discussed our routine audits and active investigations with the audit committee at our meeting this week."

"Thank you, that's helpful. I plan to start my detailed review of Margot's case files next week."

#   #   #

Friday evening, Amanda says, "I'm impressed the hosts at your neighborhood restaurants greet you by name. They all welcome you with open arms, but I would prefer to eat at home and relax. Sorry, I'm always late and haven't found time to fix dinner."

"Don't worry. Before retiring, I preferred to stay late at my office rather than take work home. I don't enjoy cooking, so I'm happy to be a regular customer at my neighborhood restaurants."

She continues, "Working in New York is not what I expected. My teammates are experienced and this is new for me. We're analyzing reports and summarizing findings from agents all over the world. I need to be at the office early and work late to keep up with them. I'm surprised Mark selected me to accompany him to Washington."

I kiss her hand, "You'll do great. It's wonderful having you in New York."

Saturday night, I'm surprised when Amanda arrives at six o'clock, "I stopped by the little grocery on my way home. I'm cooking tonight – open a red, I'm fixing Italian."

9

New York City

My career has always required juggling multiple assignments, and I enjoy the challenge of allocating time to each investigation. On Monday, I schedule my day to accommodate calls with clients, do more research on my Denver investigation, and read Margot's investigations.

Margot's first active investigation, file 20-104, describes a series of suspicious wire transfers received and sent by an offshore trading company based in Malta. She traced suspicious wire transfers received from accounts in Cyprus being sent to shell companies with accounts at American banks. Margot discussed this case with her team, Pierre's legal staff, the bank's audit committee, and Mark's team during her trip to New York.

File 20-105, concerns an employee embezzlement involving a loan officer who created a fake customer and shifted the loan proceeds to his personal account. Her notes show she planned to discuss this case with her team and assign it to a staff member after she returned from New York. I see no evidence the loan officer is aware of her suspicions and taking her laptop would not stop this investigation as all the evidence is saved on the bank's computer system.

File 20-106, outlines a potential Ponzi scheme by an Italian investment fund and her last file, 20-107, concerns a suspected fraud by a foreign financier living in Luxembourg.

# # #

Thursday morning, I call Louis. "I've completed my review of Margot's investigations. The most likely connection appears to be 20-104."

Louis responds, "I agree. The incoming wires originated from banks in Cyprus, Malta, and Eastern Europe. Our customer is an offshore trading company chartered in Malta, and all these financial transactions were allegedly for the purchase and shipping of equipment."

"The offshore firm had its account at our bank for over a year before these suspicious transactions started. We flag such firms for periodic audits, and Margot identified a series of matching wires from Cyprus this firm sent to accounts at banks in America. She told me she got curious and checked the legal status of the American firms. The companies in America all had different names, but the same legal address in a Miami strip mall. She contacted the FBI, and they arranged her meeting in New York."

I ask, "Do you think any suspects were alerted?"

"I suppose it's possible, but it's unclear what they would gain by taking Margot's laptop."

# # #

Friday morning, I receive an email from Louis:

Steve,

Pierre told me the police called him yesterday after checking the security cameras and reported they found no evidence the apartment's residents or service staff removed Margot's laptop. The police have no further plans to pursue the matter.

Any ideas?

Louis

Humm, another dead-end? If a resident or service person didn't take the laptop, then who did? Why hasn't someone tried to use her laptop? What happened to Margot's laptop?

# # #

Friday night, Amanda meets me after work at a neighborhood café. I'm feeling guilty about going to Florida and try to make amends, "Thank you, my trip to Florida for Presidents' Day was a good idea. I missed you and a little sunshine helped my attitude."

Amanda laughs, "The break was beneficial for both of us. Living day-after-day together in New York is different from spending weekends and vacations on Paradox. We both needed a break."

I smile, "I missed having you with me in Paris. Your assignment will be over in May. How about a getaway to this romantic city over Memorial Day weekend to celebrate?"

Amanda beams, "Wonderful idea!"

#   #   #

Saturday evening, Amanda says, "The task force is taking a day off tomorrow. I need some fresh air, let's take a morning walk in Central Park."

"Nice idea, I haven't done that in years."

She continues, "How was your day? Did you reach any conclusions about Margot's missing laptop?"

"No, I've read Margot's files and talked to Louis. We can think of no logical reason for anyone related to an investigation to want her laptop."

"Do you still think her death is connected?"

"I think it's unlikely she died of natural causes and it's my only clue. I hope solving the mystery of her laptop helps explain her sudden death. What if silencing Margot was the intended goal and taking her laptop was added insurance?"

10

March - New York City

I'm dreaming of Florida weather the first week of March and start scheduling my upcoming business trips to permit a few days on Paradox. I prefer to address sensitive business issues face-to-face and, as a result, have held elite airline status for decades.

I call Louis Wednesday morning. "Thanks for providing access to Margot's files. I'm stumped. The only benefit I see is for a suspect in litigation knowing what evidence is in the bank's file – but stealing her laptop won't stop an investigation or legal prosecution. I still can't think of a motive to steal her laptop. Do you have any ideas?"

Louis responds, "No, we completed our review of Margot's case notes, email and phone messages. We store all audit files on the bank's secure servers, and the legal staff monitors active investigations. Having inside knowledge of a case might help a suspect already in litigation, but they would need Margot's password to open her computer. Bank security has seen no evidence anyone has attempted to use her laptop. Margot was last online when she checked her messages after landing in Paris."

"Did you discover anything unusual when you reviewed her phone, text and email messages? Any suspicious messages or threats?"

"No, we found nothing suspicious."

I continue, "Pierre said the police examined videos from security cameras in her building. Have you looked at them?"

"Monsieur Rochat relied on the police investigation. He said they reported no suspicious activity and she was not followed into the building."

"Humm, I would like to review these items for myself. Can you add copies of the police report, the medical exam and the building's security videos to my 'read-only' account?"

#   #   #

On Friday, the student in Denver executes a new trade and purchases ten thousand dollars of stock in a small technology company. As expected, I find no rumors or announcements of a pending merger related to this company.

#   #   #

Amanda and I meet at my favorite neighborhood Mexican restaurant for dinner Friday evening. The owner seats us at a window table and serves us complimentary margaritas.

Amanda smiles, "A toast, I'm not going to the office this weekend."

I respond, "That's good news, let's put serious

conversations off-limits all weekend."

Amanda frowns, "That might be optimistic. Have you read much about Covid-19?"

"Only headlines and online reports about outbreaks in China and Italy. I'm preoccupied with Margot's death, my new Denver case, and client calls. Why do you ask?"

"Mark told us he had dinner this week with his neighbor, a hospital administrator. His neighbor is concerned about the surge of cases in Italy and expects to see more cases in New York as testing improves. Mark said it's possible we will stop holding in-person meetings at the office and most of us will start working remotely from home. Mark scheduled a meeting with us on Tuesday to develop a contingency plan."

Amanda adds, "The acronym for work-from-home is 'WFH'. Mark said it will become common usage if his neighbor is right."

I shake my head. "I've been working from the boat, hotel rooms, and my apartment for the past four years. Guess I'm a trendsetter."

11

New York City

March in New York is coming in like a lamb, and my spirits brighten on my Monday morning walk. My workday begins with reading financial news and overnight messages. Today, I'm reluctant to open a text message from an unknown number in France - until I read the first line:

"This is Marie, please call me."

Humm, I get a fresh cup of coffee and place a call to the number.

"Hello, Monsieur Wilson. Thank you for calling me."

"Please call me Steve. I hope you and your parents are well. Your call has me worried about this Covid epidemic in Europe."

"No, No, we are well. That is not the reason for my call. I've hesitated to call you, and this may not be important. My sister and I always shared our secrets and talked every few days. She was worried about something at work on our last call."

"Did she say what?"

"She said she didn't want me involved."

"Was it related to her trip to New York?"

"I don't know. She said it was a serious matter she needed to address when she returned to Paris from New York. That's all I know."

#   #   #

My first call is to Mark. "I just talked to Marie, Margot's sister. She told me Margot was worried about something at the bank, and she planned to address it when she returned to Paris. Did she mention anything to you?"

"No. What did Margot say to her sister?"

"No details, Margot didn't want her sister involved. Do you think it's related to your case?"

Mark replies, "We call Margot's analysis our Paris Connection, and it's now part of our investigation into political interference by foreign governments. Margot identified a series of suspicious wire transfers sent to shell companies established in Miami. Her investigation helped us identify illegal political contributions and advertising on social media. Margot already investigated this matter and referred it to us. She must have been referring to another problem."

I ask, "I'm uncertain how to approach Louis or Pierre with this news from Marie. Margot didn't want her sister involved. Do you have any suggestions?"

"I agree, you need to protect Marie, just follow your curious nature and ask questions."

———

# # #

It's still mid-afternoon in Paris, so I call Louis. "I'm concerned we are missing something connected to Margot's laptop. Was she worried about an old case or new investigation? Did she discuss any plans to open a new investigation with you?"

"No. She kept excellent notes, and if she thought something was suspicious, she assigned a new case number and opened an audit file. We've already examined all her notes and active investigations. I'm the new contact for 20-104, the investigation the FBI calls the Paris Connection. I have assigned all the other investigations to staff."

Louis adds, "As you requested, I contacted the police and they will not provide the bank with a copy of their internal investigation. However, building management provided me with the videos from the security cameras after I explained my position as Chief Auditor at the bank. I also learned copies of the medical examination are restricted to Margot's family."

"Thanks. I will review the security images this afternoon."

My last call is to Pierre, "I think we might be missing something. Did Margot discuss potential investigations with you?"

"She occasionally discussed potential cases with me to avoid unintended legal consequences. Her standard practice was to notify me when she opened an investigation so I could include it on the agenda for the next committee meeting. Why do you ask?"

"Just curious, I feel like we are missing something. Do you think it's possible Margot spotted something suspicious and planned to open a new investigation?"

"Not that she discussed with me."

#   #   #

Monday night, I surprise Amanda with a glass of Pinot Grigio and set the table for dinner at the apartment. However, my idea of a home-cooked meal is serving roasted chicken and vegetables delivered from a French restaurant.

She grins, "Thanks, it's been another long day and this is a treat!"

After dinner, I update Amanda on my review of the security videos from Margot's apartment building.

"The videos start with Margot's arrival at five o'clock Friday morning and end with Pierre's entrance with his assistant Monday afternoon. Each video clip is motion activated, but it took me most of the day to scan through all the activity. The videos show Margot roll her carry-on suitcase into the foyer and use the keypad to open the door into the building. Most important, she is carrying her leather laptop case. There is no other activity in the foyer until people leave for work at seven-thirty."

"The service entrance cameras show a woman departing at six o'clock and service staff start arriving at seven o'clock. People go in and out during the day carrying computer cases and packages that could conceal Margot's laptop. It's impossible to tell if anyone removed her laptop."

Amanda asks, "What do you think?"

"I think Margot did not walk into her apartment building carrying an empty computer case. Someone took her laptop."

# # #

Tuesday night, Amanda says, "We had a very educational meeting today. We are all concerned about the global spread of this new coronavirus, and we established protocols for working remotely. Mark asked us to select our preferred location and we plan to stop face-to-face meetings next week."

I'm stunned, "Whoa, what do you want to do?"

She continues, "You and I have three possible locations; New York, Palm Beach, and Portland. The desk on Paradox works for you, but the boat's not private and I can't work from the settee at the cabin table for any length of time. Your apartment isn't large enough for me to have the privacy I need for my new assignment. Finally, I can clear my desk in my alcove for you in Portland and I can work from my office. It's just a short walk from my apartment and my office space is isolated from everyone in the building."

She hesitates, "Working in Portland is best for me, but will subject you to Maine's bitterly cold weather. We could still visit Paradox for a few weekends this spring. Sorry, I just can't work full time from Paradox or the apartment in New York. What do you think?"

I'm pensive, "I don't know what to think. The news reports are confusing. This assignment is a significant opportunity for you, and your career is top priority. I don't want to stay in New York alone."

"I could work from the boat in Florida and we could try to arrange visits. I doubt your assignment will permit travel based on the past month. I could fly to Portland on weekends, but your schedule isn't predictable. The airlines are already canceling flights, so I'm not sure we can rely on air travel."

"If we want to be together, then we need to make Portland work. I have misgivings, but will try it if I can use your desk in the alcove rather than the kitchen table."

Amanda greets my answer with a wide smile, an affectionate hug, and a long kiss.

\#   \#   \#

Mark's timing is fortuitous. New testing discloses Covid-19 cases are surging in New York and the Governor announces a stay-at-home order starting next week. On Saturday, we pack up, rent a car, and drive to Portland.

12

Portland, Maine

Sunday morning, Amanda describes her plan for our new living arrangement. "I won't be working from home, so it's easy for me to clear my table desk in the alcove for you. I plan to walk to the office and my SUV will be available in the garage when you need it. I've made room in my spare closet, so you can unpack while I clear the desk."

She is smiling when I walk through the archway into her small alcove and adjust her office chair. "This chair is perfect, thank you. You were clever to have the desk face the windows; having this view of the waterfront is a luxury."

She smiles, "OK, I'll be back. I need to provision so we don't starve while being sequestered."

"OK if I explore?"

"Sure, you haven't spent much time in my apartment, make yourself at home."

Amanda's apartment is in a renovated building near Portland's downtown waterfront. Her living room, bedroom, and bathroom are all larger than my New York apartment. Amanda's décor features simple Scandinavian furniture with bright blue

53

fabrics and original watercolors of Maine's coast by local artists. My New York apartment has contemporary tan leather furniture accented with stone sculptures and prints of modern art.

# # #

Freezing rain is hitting the windows Monday morning when Amanda puts on her facemask, bright red winter coat, and matching stocking hat. She says, "I'll be home by seven to fix dinner."

I kiss her on the forehead, "You're tough, no morning walk for me."

The morning news is depressing. New York's lockdown is unprecedented, and I add tracking Covid case reports to my regular morning review of online financial news.

The stock exchanges are open, even though many employees now work from home. An acquisition announcement on Monday results in a six-thousand-dollar gain for the Denver college student. I expect Logan will sell the shares tomorrow and transfer the proceeds to his money market account.

Amanda returns at seven-thirty and sets her leather backpack on the chair, removes her coat, hat, black leather boots, facemask and kisses me. "Sorry, I'm late. I'll have haddock with pasta ready in thirty minutes. How was your day?"

"My day was fine. Take a break, let's share a glass of Chardonnay before you head to the galley."

We touch glasses and move to the sofa. Amanda

sighs, "Whew, it's been a long day. Thanks!"

#   #   #

We can't discuss Amanda's assignment, so our evening conversations focus on my investigations.

Tuesday, I say, "Logan completed his fourteenth merger trade yesterday and sold the shares today. I've added all the names related to this transaction to my computer analysis, but the program still fails to isolate a single source of inside information. Logan's total profits over the past year now exceed sixty-thousand-dollars. I'm baffled."

#   #   #

Louis calls on Wednesday. "Your suggestions are making my transition to day-to-day management much easier. I hope you don't mind my frequent calls."

"Not at all, I'm glad to help."

He says, "I've been thinking about anything unusual we might have missed. I need to mention a call I received from a bank in Lausanne the week after Margot died. The account officer told me a wire Margot asked about should be disregarded as it was sent in error and the entry reversed. I assumed the matter was resolved."

"Do you have a copy of that wire? Was it related to her visit to New York? I don't remember seeing a wire from Switzerland."

"There is no wire from the Lausanne bank in our New York file."

"Why not call him back?"

"I did. I checked my phone log and placed a call to the bank. The man who answered said he didn't remember the wire, so it must have been a routine matter."

Louis pauses, "I did a computer scan yesterday and didn't find any reference to this inquiry in Margot's files. So, I checked her phone log. She called this same number the week before she went to New York, but I can't find a note in any file. That's unusual, Margot documented everything."

# # #

Pierre calls the following day. "France has restricted all non-essential travel in response to this global pandemic, and we are shifting our April audit committee meeting to a video conference. I plan to recommend Louis to become our Chief Auditor and we want you to take part in our virtual meeting to endorse his selection."

"I'll be happy to do so. Louis is doing a professional job. He has an excellent educational background, solid professional credentials, and fifteen years of bank audit experience. He is clearly qualified to be your new Chief Auditor."

# # #

Amanda departs for her Portland office before sunrise each day and attempts to return home at seven o'clock to prepare dinner. I'm glad she likes to cook; Maine's Governor has ordered all bars to close and restaurants are restricted to takeout orders due to the Covid pandemic. Fortunately,

Maine's emergency stay-at-home order permits my morning walks for exercise.

Amanda expresses a sigh of relief when she arrives home Friday night. "This week has gone better than I expected. The video conference system works well for our team. My office is a safe space for me to work and we agree sweaters and jeans are acceptable for working remotely. I enjoy being at home, cooking in my kitchen, and appreciate your willingness to endure this frigid weather."

She pauses, "I hope our arrangement is working for you."

"It's taking time to adjust, but the desk in your alcove works for me and your waterfront view is spectacular. It's much better than looking into office building windows across the street from my apartment."

Portland Waterfront

"I'm fascinated by watching the activity on the lobster boats on my morning walk. I'm impressed, those lobstermen go out to pull their traps in all kinds of weather. This morning's fog was so dense I couldn't see the boats once they pulled away from the dock."

I pause, "However, this March weather feels surprisingly frigid. It's frustrating staying inside most of the day, but I feel silly complaining. It sounds like most of the county will soon be in lockdown with stay-at-home orders. At least, we are together and my work keeps me focused."

I continue, "On the plus side, being sequestered has given me more time to edit *Synthetic Escape*. I'm ready for you to read my proof copy when you have time. I hope to publish my new book next month."

She smiles, "Absolutely, I need to go to the office tomorrow, but I welcome a change of topic to clear my brain on Sunday. I'll accept a backrub as payment."

13

Portland, Maine

The last week of March is still too damn cold for me and I complain again at dinner Tuesday evening. "I didn't realize how much colder it would feel in Maine. I find it difficult to enjoy my morning walk."

Amanda grins, "How did you tolerate winters living in Chicago and New York?"

"Good question, that seems an eternity ago. I haven't owned a car since I moved to Chicago thirty years ago. That's when I first moved into a high-rise apartment building and started walking to work. I frequently stopped at a gym in the morning to exercise before going to my office. I spent most of my time at the bank, eating in restaurants, or walking through airports. I feel trapped in your apartment. I need longer walks for exercise with the gyms closed."

I pause, "Sorry, I don't mean to complain. I've never spent day-after-day inside any apartment. I miss being able to treat you to dinner at Portland's world-class restaurants. Damn, this is only our second week in Portland, and I'm already getting cabin fever."

#   #   #

On Wednesday, I call Pierre, "I'm still thinking about Margot's laptop. Building management was kind enough to send the security videos to Louis. What did the police tell you about the woman wearing the fedora who departed the service entrance that morning?"

Pierre laughs, "The police found the situation amusing. They told me their inquiries made a married man very nervous and, with no evidence of a crime, they saw no reason to interfere in his extra-marital affairs."

"I see, thank you."

#   #   #

On Thursday, I decide it's time to broach an uncomfortable topic and call Marie to ask for a copy of Margot's medical exam.

She sighs, "I will see what I can do. The medical report was sent to my parents and I'm reluctant to ask them for a copy. I work as a fashion designer at a specialty shop in Paris, and our shop is closed due to this pandemic. It's a hard time for me."

"Sorry, I don't want to trouble you."

#   #   #

Friday night, Amanda prepares another delightful Italian dinner and asks, "You feeling any better? I hope being sequestered with me in Portland is working better."

"Yes, I'm glad we're together. I'm adjusting to my new daily routine and my clients keep me busy. My banking contacts call every day asking about enhancing online security for employees working on their personal devices from home. This is not my specialty, but the national firms are overwhelmed and many of their employees are also working from home. All banks have backup plans for natural disasters, but this pandemic presents a new nationwide opportunity for phishing schemes and cyberattacks."

Amanda says, "Reports of phishing attacks on business systems have surged with employees working from home. A few years ago, these attacks were by freelancers using fake emails to steal personal information. Criminals still post stolen credit card, bank account, social security, passport, and other types of information for sale on the dark web."

She continues, "Today's cybercriminals are more sophisticated and target individuals, corporations, and governments with phishing schemes designed to plant malware to steal and block access to computer files. Today, they get quicker paybacks by charging ransom to unlock blocked systems and they still sell the stolen information."

She pauses, "I'm glad you're adjusting. Have you learned anything new about Margot's laptop?"

"No. I found time in between my client calls to review the videos from the security cameras again. The cameras recorded no activity after Margot arrived until a woman with dark hair wearing a fedora departs the service entrance at six o'clock. Service staff starts arriving at seven o'clock and residents start for work at seven-thirty."

"I called Pierre to ask about the woman who departed at six. I was curious because the small overnight bag she carried is large enough to conceal Margot's laptop. He told me the police identified her as the guest of a married man while his wife was out of town."

"The security camera is above the keypad and I've downloaded her photo."

Amanda winks, "Clever, she used her fedora to cover most of her face while sneaking out the back door. Any update on Margot's medical exam?"

"I've hesitated to ask Marie about the medical exam but called her yesterday. She's reluctant to ask her parents for a copy."

14

April - Portland, Maine

Maine's Governor extends her stay-at-home order for April. Most of the country is now in lockdown except for essential services.

Amanda removes her facemask and complains as she walks into her apartment Monday evening. "Shopping is a nightmare; everyone is stocking up at Hannaford's. The paper product shelves are still empty; not a roll of paper towels or toilet paper in sight. I could only buy a few cans of soup for your lunch. I need to go back tomorrow morning."

"Hey. I can shop, just make a list."

"Thanks, take your facemask and bundle up, you may need to stand in a line outside. The store restricts the number of people inside and everyone is social distancing, wearing a facemask, and using the hand sanitizer at the door before they enter."

"No problem, the L.L.Bean sweaters and winter coat you bought me have made a vast difference and I'm tolerating this weather. I'll make the store my destination rather than walk along the waterfront. I can't believe it's still this cold. When does spring start?"

She smiles, "Next month if we're lucky."

I say, "We need to stay safe, but being restricted to my morning walks and video calls is frustrating. I never expected to miss airports, but I prefer traveling and meeting people face-to-face."

Amanda agrees, "These Covid restrictions are frustrating and the nightly news is too depressing to watch. I can't discuss my assignment, so our nightly conversations focus on your activities. We need a break, let's stream a movie after dinner."

#   #   #

I'm wearing jeans with my pinstripe suit coat and nautical tie when Amanda walks in Wednesday night. She looks puzzled when she sees me arranging 3x5 index cards on the living room coffee table.

"What are you doing?"

"Oh, I got distracted with my Denver analysis after my video conference. I've entered every name associated with these mergers into my computer program. My software identifies potential links between the firms and people related to all the mergers, but the diagrams it creates for this investigation are useless. I've regressed to using these 3x5 cards to help me visualize potential connections."

"Any progress?"

"Not yet. I've been working on this case for two months and my client is getting restless."

# # #

Friday night, Amanda asks, "I'm curious. How are your banking clients coping with customer service?"

"It's a tough situation. Banks provide essential services and need to stay open. My clients are concerned about the safety of their staff and most are restricting service to drive-thru windows and require facemasks for limited office appointments."

Amanda says, "I have growing admiration for all the people who risk their health by going to work every day. Bank tellers, grocery store check-out clerks, mail carriers, truck drivers, delivery services, and police are all out there doing their jobs. Health care professionals are the front line. It's hard to believe we have a shortage of personal protective equipment for doctors, nurses, and hospital support staff. The media is right, these people are heroes."

I add, "I don't want to sound pessimistic, but the growing number of hospitalizations and deaths is depressing. I don't see how we can return to normal activities without some miracle therapy or vaccine."

"I agree. Mark told us today we should plan on working remotely for the foreseeable future. So, you and I need to talk about our summer plans."

I laugh, "Summer plans? How can we make plans with this much uncertainly?"

Amanda smiles, "OK, Mr. Pessimist. I have an idea."

"Let's hear it. I need a more positive outlook."

Amanda explains, "The boatyards can remain open if they adhere to safety guidelines. Vendors and customers are not allowed inside their buildings, but their crews are performing repairs and doing routine maintenance in anticipation of summer cruising. Being on a boat this summer will be a great way to social distance and we should expect boating activity will be permitted."

"OK, but Paradox is in Florida and I'm not planning airline travel anytime soon."

She continues, "I've been thinking about buying a boat we could use in the summer, but my assignment and these safety restrictions make it impossible for me to look at boats today."

She smiles, "So...............why not put Paradox on a truck and bring her to Maine?"

I cheer up, "Interesting idea – who should I call?"

"I already have – I called Justin at Front Street Shipyard in Belfast and he can have Paradox shipped to them in May. What do you think?"

I lean over and give her a kiss. "I think you're amazing!"

15

Portland, Maine

The prospect of having Paradox in Maine for the summer brightens my spirits. On Monday, I call Justin and confirm the truck will bring Paradox to Front Street Shipyard in mid-May.

# # #

The Paris bank's virtual audit committee meeting is Wednesday. I wear jeans but select a nautical tie, white dress shirt, and a blue suit coat for the camera. As planned, they call me to endorse Pierre's recommendation to select Louis as the bank's new Chief Auditor.

The next morning, I receive a call from Louis. "Thank you. I appreciate your advice and support. Margot was right, you are a great mentor and I hope you will be available for future help."

I'm self-conscious, "Thank you, you are very kind. No problem, you can call me anytime."

The following day, I receive a call from Pierre, "The committee and I appreciate your input on our succession decision. Louis updated the committee on Margot's missing laptop, and they concluded no further reports are necessary unless we detect an attempt to access bank systems. Sebastian Hedinger asked me to extend his appreciation to you as your services are no longer needed."

"No problem, glad to be of service. I will let you know if I have any new ideas concerning Margot's laptop."

# # #

I'm still playing with my 3x5 cards when Amanda walks in Friday night. She asks, "Any progress?"

"Not sure. This isn't a typical insider trading scheme with a single source of information. Somehow, I need to isolate multiple sources."

# # #

Amanda stays home Sunday. We sleep late and she prepares a lobster omelet for brunch. The afternoon weather is warmer, so we put on our facemasks and walk hand-in-hand along the waterfront.

Our walk takes us by one of our favorite restaurants. I say, "It's sad to see the restaurants closed. This is the first time in decades I can remember eating every meal at home. Our forced sequester has made me appreciate your culinary skills. I don't think you've duplicated a meal. I don't see any cookbooks, how do you do it?"

Amanda laughs, "Thanks, I enjoy cooking and experimenting with different ingredients. I never know what dinner will be until I look in the refrigerator."

She continues, "Before Covid, I met girlfriends after work for drinks and dinner about twice a month. Otherwise, I seldom ate at restaurants unless it was business or I was with you. I was surprised you went to restaurants for every meal."

I object, "That's not fair! I'm fixing my breakfast and lunch."

Amanda laughs, "I appreciate your help today, but a bowl of cereal, bagels and cream cheese, a couple of donuts or soup from a can hardly qualify as gourmet cooking."

I'm defeated, "OK, you got a point."

16

Portland, Maine

The third week of April begins with an unexpected call from Mark.

"The task force has identified a link between Margot's case and our ransomware project. Amanda tracked some ransomware proceeds to the accounts investigated by Margot."

"I think you might offer a fresh set of eyes on this relationship. I'm activating your consulting agreement and will authorize Amanda to share information about this Paris Connection with you. You and Amanda can talk about this relationship, but the rest of the task force's investigation remains off-limits."

#   #   #

Amanda is serious when she enters the apartment, "Mark told me he activated your consulting agreement today and we can talk about the Paris Connection. He thinks you might uncover a link between our case and Margot's death."

I shake my head, "I still don't see any reason to kill Margot. What's new about this connection?"

"We traced funds from ransomware attacks to accounts in Cyprus and one of the account numbers matches the wire transfers investigated by Margot. The funds from the Cyprus account were sent to the Paris bank and then to accounts opened by shell companies in Miami to purchase political advertising on social media."

She pauses, "Foreign governments are using cyberattacks and domestic ransom payments to disrupt our elections."

"Have you identified the people or nations behind the ransomware attack?"

"Yes, but that's classified information."

I'm perplexed, "What am I supposed to do? Can I share my new involvement with Pierre and Louis?"

"Yes, if there is a connection to Margot's death then Mark and I expect your inquiring mind will uncover it."

#   #   #

The next morning, I call Pierre to explain my involvement. I'm pleased when he replies;

"Yes, I've been expecting your call. Louis updated me on the investigation last night. We both welcome your official involvement. What can we do to help?"

"I don't know, do you have any recent information to share?"

"I don't think so. Louis will keep you up-to-date

and he is expecting your call."

# # #

Louis says, "I'm glad we now have an official relationship on this investigation and I will create a new 'read-only' file for you. I'll brief the audit committee at our next meeting."

# # #

On Wednesday, I receive an email from Marie:

Steve,

I visited my parents' home last weekend. It was awkward. We all wore facemasks, kept our distance, and didn't hug or touch.

Mother placed an unopened envelope with Margot's medical exam on the dining table. My parents don't have a scanner, so I opened it and took photos of each page with my phone. Please don't share this with anyone.

She also gave me three boxes of books and papers the bank sent from Margot's apartment. Mother asked me to see if there is anything important, so I brought the boxes back to Paris with me.

We are still grieving - this was a sad visit. I need to keep them safe, hated not embracing, and cried all the way back to Paris.

Marie

I download the photos and scan through the exam. Tears fill my eyes when I see the medical examiner's pictures of Margot on a stainless-steel table. I close my laptop. I can't do this today.

# # #

The following day, I receive a text from Louis with a new password for access to a 'read-only' file of documents related to the Paris Connection.

Friday night, I update Amanda. "I received 'read-only' access to the bank's files yesterday and see little new information. Your communications with the bank contain redacted information, lots of text is blacked out. Will I have access to that information?"

"No, it's classified."

# # #

Amanda prepares pancakes with bacon and eggs on Sunday morning before we take a walk along Portland's waterfront to enjoy a sunny day.

She is quiet on our walk and I ask, "Is everything OK? You seem preoccupied."

"Sorry, I talked with a friend yesterday who works for social services. She shared her concerns about the unintended consequences of this pandemic lockdown. I was thinking about the calls she's been receiving from women reporting spousal and child abuse. It's a terrible situation when unhappy families are stuck together inside with no prospect of returning to work."

I give her a hug and soft kiss, "I'm lucky to be sequestering with the woman I love."

17

Portland, Maine

Monday morning, my hands are shaking when I click 'open' to read Margot's medical exam. I try to control my emotions, but tears run down my cheek as I look at the photos. An hour later, I close the file, wipe away tears, and call Mark.

"I just finished reading Margot's medical exam and was shocked when the report said an empty bottle of sleep medication was on her bed and the police suspected suicide. However, the medical exam only found a non-lethal level of sleeping medication in her system. The only other toxicology test was for illegal drugs and none were found."

"The medical examiner said no sign of drugs nor trauma contributed to her death, and he concluded she died from natural causes. The police had no reason to suspect a crime so a forensic autopsy was not requested."

Mark says, "I see; they closed the case when it wasn't death by suicide, drugs, or trauma."

I continue, "The photos show a small bruise on the right side of her neck and three broken fingernails on her right hand. Did you notice a bruise or broken fingernails when she was in New York?"

"No, but I'll ask the team if they noticed. Did you see anything else in the photos?"

"No." I pause, "It's very hard to look at them."

# # #

Amanda walks in Monday evening and sees my sullen mood. "What's wrong? You look troubled."

"I read Margot's medical exam today and the photos are disturbing."

"I'm sorry, anything I can do?"

"No, I called Mark today and told him it's not what I expected. It was a superficial medical procedure as the police had no reason to suspect a crime had been committed."

"The medical exam mentioned a small bruise and three broken fingernails. I still choke-up when I think about her photos. Mark doesn't remember a bruise or broken fingernails and he is checking with the team members that met with Margot. I suspect the fingernails were broken after she returned to Paris."

"Why? What do you suspect?"

"Margot held an important management position and was always very careful about looking and acting professionally. I can't believe she would go anywhere with the three broken fingernails shown in the photo."

Amanda says, "Have you considered she could have broken them on the return flight or at the

75

airport retrieving her suitcase? It's happened to me."

"What about the bruise?"

"Can I look at the photos?"

I hesitate, "Not today. Marie asked that I not share the report and I want to respect her wishes. You and Mark are the only people who know I have a copy."

"What's next?"

"Pierre had all the conversations with the police and I plan to call him tomorrow. I'm not going to mention the medical exam, but want to ask him again about his conversations."

#   #   #

"Bonjour Pierre. If you have time, I want to ask a few more questions about Margot."

"Certainly, may I assume this is related to what your FBI calls the Paris Connection?"

"Yes, I'm still concerned about a connection between this investigation and Margot's missing laptop."

Pierre sighs, "I thought this was settled. What do you want to ask?"

"Did the Police take any DNA or fingerprints from Margot's apartment?"

Pierre hesitates, "Monsieur Wilson, remember, the

police found an empty bottle of sleeping medication next to her on the bed. They were initially certain Margot's death was suicide and requested a medical exam to confirm their suspicions. I was relieved when they said the medical examiner reported natural causes. I didn't want to risk harming Margot's reputation by mentioning suicide. I hope you understand."

"Thank you, I understand."

# # #

Tuesday evening, Amanda asks, "Did you learn anything new from Pierre?"

"The police told him they suspected suicide. He was relieved when natural causes were reported as the official cause of death, and he didn't share their suspicions of suicide with anyone."

I continue, "I'm perplexed, I can't ask him about Margot's broken fingernails without telling him I have a copy of the medical examination. Marie asked me to keep it private."

"What did he say about fingerprints or DNA?"

I hesitate, "He didn't – he shared the police suspicions about suicide."

"Any other ideas? What about the security videos?"

"Humm…… interesting idea. Let's look."

I open my laptop to the file with security videos from Margot's apartment building.

I say, "The building's security system works with motion activated cameras facing the entrance to the security vestibule, the door into the building, and a camera over the keypad. This video into the building shows the keypad over her shoulder. Let's see if we can stop action with a clear shot of her right hand."

Amanda smiles, "Good job, she was right-handed and you can see her reach for the passcode keypad. Can you zoom in?"

"Yes. Her fingernails look fine to me."

Amanda asks, "What about the bruise?"

"I can't tell. Her long hair covers the space below her ear from this angle."

Amanda looks at me, "Well done. This confirms Margot's fingernails were broken after she returned to her apartment."

18

May – Portland, Maine

May begins the same way April ends. Maine's Governor extends her stay-at-home order to mid-June, and she requires anyone coming into the state to quarantine for two weeks.

#   #   #

Amanda arrives home on Tuesday, "Still playing with your cards?"

"Don't laugh, I solved the puzzle."

"You identified the inside source?"

"Not yet, but this college student is getting stock tips that trace back to three different firms. Logan has more than one inside source."

"How could a college student in Denver have that many insider contacts in New York?"

"I don't know. I've been rearranging these cards for weeks. I started looking for a single connection to all the acquisitions and always ended up with extra cards."

"I changed my approach a month ago and started

---

arranging the cards into separate stacks by potential contacts instead of looking for a single contact with a relationship to all of Logan's investments."

"OK, and what did you learn?"

"This afternoon, I reduced the number of stacks to three firms. It's not one insider source, somehow this college student has an inside source at two investment banking firms and one law firm."

"That's incredible. What's next?"

"I don't think Logan has three separate insider contacts; most likely he has a contact with connections to three inside sources."

"How do you plan to identify this contact and these inside sources? You don't have enough evidence to obtain a court order to search his computer, phone, email, and text messages."

"That's right, but he is active on social media. My next step is sorting through his social media friends and isolating people who have relationships with these three Wall Street firms."

I continue, "He hasn't made a trade since the New York lockdown, so I think his insider sources are restricted by New York's stay-at-home order. I remember a situation about ten years ago. Home burglaries were occurring when our bank's officers were traveling with their wives. The thieves parked a fake delivery truck in their driveway and stole everything of value. Somehow, the thieves knew the house was unoccupied, so we started looking for a common link."

"A travel agent. Right?"

"First place we looked, and it was a dead end."

"OK, I'm listening."

"There was a barbershop in the bank tower and we traced the common link to a 'friendly' barber. I remember the guy as a real 'chatterbox' and he complained about never going anywhere. He said he always wanted to travel and asked me and other bank officers about our favorite places and upcoming trips. He conspired with two other men and they robbed executive homes based on his travel information."

"What's your point?"

"Logan's insider trades stopped when New York locked down, so I suspect his information is restricted by the lockdown. Maybe they frequent a business that stopped serving Wall Street customers - like a barbershop, gym, restaurant, or bar. My next step is to research each of his friends and see where they work."

#   #   #

Wednesday morning, I receive an unexpected call from Louis. "I am required to present a year-to-date summary of our audits twice a year for the audit committee. My first report is due in June and I started preparing the summary this week. I discovered something strange – Margot skipped a potential case number."

He continues, "Bank policy requires us to perform an annual audit of expense accounts and review the financial accounts for the bank's executive officers. We start our annual reviews in December and report our results covering the prior year to the audit committee at their January meeting. Margot established Case 20-101 for this project. The committee requested no follow-up action at the meeting and the file was closed."

"We also collect forms submitted by members of our board of directors listing any potential conflict of interest. Margot established Case 20-102 for this project, and we provided a summary and copies of these reports to our audit committee for their review in January. Again, the committee requested no follow-up action, and the file was closed."

"The next file in our system is Case 20-104, the first active investigation we shared with you. There is no record Margot established Case 20-103. I find it difficult to believe she got confused and skipped a number. What do you think?"

I'm stumped, "I don't know what to think. Margot was always precise and she didn't make careless errors. This makes little sense. Is it possible for someone to delete a file?"

"We can edit information during an investigation, but everything is frozen after an audit file is closed. All files require a password and we save deleted documents for six months after an audit or investigation is completed."

"What date was Case 20-102 closed and when was Case 20-104 established?"

"Let me see, 20-101 and 20-102 were both closed on Friday, January 17th, the day after the audit committee meeting. Case 20-104 was opened Monday, January 20th, the day before Margot went to New York."

"Why don't you ask your cybersecurity staff to examine Margot's files between those dates to see if they detect any suspicious activity. I'm curious if her laptop and this missing case file are connected."

"We've already checked activity on her active case files and there was nothing suspicious. I will ask security to do a system search for Case 20-103. I'll keep you informed."

#   #   #

Two days later, I receive an email from Louis:

Steve,

Our cybersecurity team completed their analysis. There is no evidence Case 20-103 ever existed.

Louis

Damn, another dead-end?

19

Portland, Maine

Amanda removes her blue nautical jacket and facemask when she arrives home Monday night. I have a glass of Chardonnay waiting and say, "Cheers, hope you had a good day."

"I did. It was awkward at first, but we've adjusted to spending most of the day discussing our analysis on a secure video call rather than working around a conference table in New York. Our encrypted network provides access to the same information we had in New York. My teammates are both working from home and we all seem more relaxed wearing jeans. How about you?"

I say, "I'm ready for a glass of wine. Searching social media accounts is tedious, but I'm fascinated by the variety of Logan's friends."

We tap our glasses and move to the living room sofa. "I only join social networks to promote my mystery novels. Logan is online every day, and he has accumulated over seven hundred friends across several social media platforms. Pre-pandemic, Logan and his friends posted photos at restaurants, clubs, parties, museums, sporting events, and outdoor activities. Today, they mostly share old photos and jokes."

Amanda's puzzled, "I don't use social media. My family and friends use email and talk on the phone. How much can you learn about Logan's friends?"

"Most of these social media accounts are public, so I can view their profiles, text posts, and photos. The amount of personal information Logan and his social media friends share for strangers to view online is staggering."

#   #   #

On Wednesday, a call from Pierre interrupts my social media analysis.

"Steve, I have sad news. A hit-and-run driver killed Louis last night outside his apartment. He has been working from home and his wife said he went out to buy groceries. It was just after dark and the police told me they have a vague description of the woman driver from the only witness."

"His neighborhood is generally quite busy, but most establishments are closed due to the pandemic. The police are viewing security cameras from the area to see if they can identify the car and driver."

"The bank provides insurance for our employees and Louis's wife should be financially secure. They had no children. That's all I know today."

"I don't know what to say. This is tragic."

"I'll let you know when I learn more."

"Thank you."

#   #   #

I call Mark after my call from Pierre. "I have bad news. Louis was killed by a hit-and-run driver in Paris last night."

"I already know; Pierre called me first and asked me to give him time to give you the sad news. Should I call Amanda or do you want to tell her?"

"Let me, thanks."

"What's wrong?" are Amanda's first words when she enters the apartment.

#   #   #

Pierre calls the following day. "The police located neighborhood security video of the accident. They found the car but not the woman driver. The car was stolen the day before the accident, so that's why she didn't stop. They discovered two empty vodka bottles inside the car and assume the driver was under the influence. They have taken multiple fingerprints from the car. Sadly, they are not confident they will locate the driver."

He pauses, "I have a dilemma. Louis did not have an assistant ready to manage the audit function. Sebastian asked me to contact you for advice. This pandemic makes it very difficult to start a search and conduct interviews. I've offered to supervise the audit department on a temporary basis. Does this seem logical to you?"

I reply, "I only communicated with Louis and don't know his staff. Providing daily oversight is probably your only alternative at present. Chief Auditor is an essential position and you are already busy. The audit committee should retain a search firm

―

immediately or you will never sleep."

I hear Pierre sigh. "I agree. Assuming this audit responsibility will be a burden for me, but necessary. Is it OK if I tell Sebastian you support this arrangement?"

"Sure, on a short-term basis."

"Thank you."

20

Portland, Maine

Amanda and I don our facemasks Sunday morning and take a breezy waterfront walk to pick up lobster rolls from the new takeout window at a favorite restaurant. Maine's lockdown restricts business activity, the stores are closed and the streets are deserted. Amanda says, "These quiet waterfront streets feel post-apocalyptic, we need to stream a comedy after lunch to cheer us up."

Sunday evening, she asks, "Do you want to watch another movie after dinner?"

"I don't think so. Thanks for trying to distract me, but I'm preoccupied with Louis's accident. It's hard to believe both Margot and Louis are dead."

"Do you think their deaths are related?"

"It's probably a coincidence, but I want to learn more about his accident."

#   #   #

Monday morning, I call Pierre. "I'm curious. Is it possible for you to send me copies of the camera footage that recorded the accident?"

"I doubt the police will provide it to me. They are very reluctant to share potential evidence. I will let you know if this is possible."

"Thank you."

# # #

My ability to read French is much better than my speaking skills. In any event, computer programs do an excellent job of translating text, and I search Paris newspapers for information about hit-and-run accidents. I'm rewarded with an online article and a photo!

The translation software reads:

The driver of a stolen car lost control and drove up on a sidewalk, killing a pedestrian. A witness says the driver was a woman with dark hair, wearing a facemask and a large hat. The accident victim was hit from behind and killed while walking to a nearby grocery. The police are asking the public to help locate this stolen car and its driver.

The blurry news photo shows the car up on the narrow sidewalk just a few feet behind Louis.

Monday evening, Amanda walks in with a bag of groceries. I say, "Welcome home. I would like you to look at this photo before you get comfortable."

"Sure, may I ask why?"

"Just look, what do you see?"

"A very careless driver or something intentional. What is this?"

"It's the photo from a news report about Louis's accidental death."

Amanda takes a second look, "What does the story say about the car and driver?"

"The car was stolen and the police think the woman driver was under the influence of alcohol."

#   #   #

The next morning, I call Pierre. "I discovered an online newspaper story with a photo describing Louis's accident. The news photo is disturbing. The driver of the car appears to be aiming at Louis. Have the police suggested this might have been intentional?"

"No, they told me they suspect the driver of the stolen car was under the influence of alcohol. They found empty bottles and the car smelled of vodka."

"Why don't you tell them Louis was a bank auditor working on very sensitive matters? Ask if they considered intentional homicide."

"Monsieur Wilson, I'll inquire with the police, but don't you think you're being a bit melodramatic?"

#   #   #

Amanda arrives home Friday evening smiling like a cat, "This week wraps up my official assignment. Mark submitted our report last week and the Congressional Committee seemed pleased with Mark's virtual presentation this morning."

She shakes her head. "It's only been a couple of

hours since his presentation and highlights of our classified report describing recent attacks by hostile foreign governments are already being leaked to the press."

I give her a hug. "Well done! You certainly kept the congressional meeting secret from me. Any information you can share?"

"No names, but we analyzed information from the FBI, CIA, and Treasury Department. Our focus was to follow the money and identify any foreign governments sponsoring these attacks. A few talented programmers can disguise their location and steal information from around the world. They target military secrets, political activity, corporate technology, and personal information. This year, we've seen a wave of malware schemes meant to steal information about the development and production of coronavirus vaccines."

"This calls for Champagne. When do you resume your responsibilities for Maine?"

She grins, "I don't. Mark asked me to join his staff in New York and work with agents across the country. He expects my job will require extensive travel, but I will continue to work from home until Covid is under control."

We share a long embrace. "I'm not surprised. I knew you would do an outstanding job as his representative on the task force."

"Thanks, my first assignment is to follow-up on two domestic ransomware schemes we uncovered."

"What about the Paris Connection?"

"Our job was to identify hostile governments behind cyber and ransomware attacks and follow the flow of money. We identified the country behind the Paris Connection in our classified report, and Margot's investigation stopped the flow of money into illegal political donations and social media advertising. Treasury plans to announce sanctions on several of this nation's leaders and our official investigation is closed."

"It's closed? What about Margot's laptop and the circumstances of her death?"

"Our investigation is closed, but there is nothing to stop your personal inquiry. Mark and I both know your curiosity is not satisfied."

"Humm......... OK. I'll be back, I need to buy a bottle of Champagne so we can celebrate your success!"

21

Portland, Maine

My outlook improves the last week of May - no jacket required for my morning walk. I give Amanda a big hug and kiss when she returns home Monday night, "Paradox arrived at Front Street today and they will have her waiting at the marina's dock when I arrive next week!"

At dinner, we both try to avoid talking about the pandemic and discuss ideas for summer cruising. Amanda says, "Even with summer traffic, Boothbay Harbor is less than a two-hour drive from Portland and works best for my weekend visits. I'm disappointed Covid restrictions forced us to cancel our plans for a Paris holiday, but we can plan for my official two-week vacation at the end of August. What do you think?"

I reply, "Boothbay works for me. I'm just happy to be with you and have Paradox in Maine for the summer."

#   #   #

Tuesday evening, Amanda says, "We filed charges today against two college students in Florida. They were masking their location by using servers in eastern Europe to launch ransomware attacks."

"Once they compromised a computer system, they rotated server locations to demand ransom paid in bitcoin. They were using public WiFi networks to communicate by email and lost their connection to the remote servers on occasion."

"That was our break, and we isolated three ransom emails sent from a national fast-food location in Gainesville. Inside dining at this location is closed, but they keep videos of cars in the drive-thru. We obtained a court order and compiled a list of drive-thru auto tag numbers for that time period."

"We tracked ransomware email back to this location's WiFi on three separate occasions. I used tag numbers to identify four cars visiting this location at each of those times. Our local agent located and arranged video calls with each of the drivers. When confronted with the photos, one of the drivers admitted to driving his friend to the fast-food outlet. He said his friend bought him lunch while they used the WiFi for social media in the parking lot."

"After this interview, we had sufficient evidence to obtain a search warrant to examine their online activity. These two college students were treating blackmail as a computer game to see who could accumulate the most bitcoin. They weren't even spending the money."

"The case is now in the hands of our attorneys and they want to set an example. They plan to seek both fines and jail time."

#　　#　　#

Wednesday night, I share my daily activity with

Amanda. "My banking clients are adjusting to their state's pandemic safety protocols. My video conferences are shifting from cybersecurity policy to discussing compliance with the new government lending programs. These well-intended business assistance programs lack the documentation required for bank compliance. We all understand Congress and governmental agencies will not take responsibility for any future problems."

#   #   #

On Thursday, Amanda observes, "You look tired and frustrated, what's wrong?"

"Just a tedious day reading social media profiles and posts. Logan is from Minneapolis, received his undergraduate degree in history from Columbia in New York, and is pursuing his masters in Denver. He has accumulated over seven hundred friends on social media. Each of Logan's friends has hundreds of social media friends. This method of identifying his potential Wall Street contacts is a nightmare, and I'm still working my way through his friends."

"So far, I've identified several dozen connections enrolled in colleges in New York. Their social media pages show all but two returned home after their schools discontinued in-person classes. I don't see any obvious connections to Wall Street for any of these college students."

"The good news is I've isolated fifteen of Logan's friends who work at investment banking firms or law firms in New York. I plan to research these connections after I go to Paradox next week."

"Logan's older sister, Ashley, graduated with an art

degree from Columbia two years ago and she was working in a restaurant in the city before the lockdown. She has over a thousand friends and posts photos almost every day."

I pause, "My client in Denver is getting impatient. This investigation is more complex and is taking much longer than I expected."

Amanda kisses me on the neck and says, "You need a break, get your mask, and let's take an evening stroll through Lincoln Park. The lilacs are blooming."

22

June – Belfast, Maine/Aboard Paradox

The logistics to drive to Belfast, organize the boat, and move Paradox to Boothbay Harbor are complex. Amanda drives me to Portland's Jetport to pick up my rental car on Sunday evening. The rental car location in Belfast is closed due to the pandemic, but their Bangor office said I can return the car and drop the keys in the Belfast lockbox.

I drive to Belfast on Monday and call Amanda. "Front Street's crew had Paradox waiting for me at the dock. They cleaned the road grime from her hull and cabin top and, as promised, she was sparkling in the morning sunlight when I arrived."

Paradox Arrives at Front Street Shipyard

Monday evening, I report my progress to Amanda.

"It's been a good day. The interior is clean and organized. My computer, communication systems, navigation software, and the boat's equipment are tested and working properly. I'm ready for dinner."

"What's on your menu?"

I laugh, "I stopped at Hannaford's to buy coffee, cereal, blueberries, milk, vegetable soup, and a frozen chicken pasta dinner. I plan to provision for the week tomorrow morning. I also need to visit Hamilton's marine store and will return the rental car Wednesday morning."

She asks, "How about Covid? Are people following the safety protocols in Belfast?"

"Yes. It feels strange not shaking hands and keeping socially distanced from Justin and the boatyard crew. I took a walk this afternoon and signs posted along the public walkway and in the restaurants and stores remind everyone to wear masks and social distance."

"Restaurants and coffee shops have added sidewalk picnic tables and takeout. Facemasks are required to enter any establishment. I'm impressed, nearly everyone is wearing their masks outdoors along the waterfront's public walkway."

"Any progress on your social media project?"

"Not today. These people post something every day, but I hope to narrow down my suspects by the end of the week."

"Do you still plan to go to Boothbay this weekend?"

"Yes. The weather looks good and I've emailed Kim to plan on my Sunday arrival."

#   #   #

On Thursday, I receive an unexpected call from Sebastian Hedinger, Chair of the Paris bank's audit committee.

"Monsieur Wilson, our committee is impressed with your credentials and we appreciated your opinion concerning our selection of Louis as Chief Auditor. Several members of my committee think it's time we start our search for his replacement and they asked me to contact you. They want to know if you can recommend a search firm."

I hesitate, "I'm confused by your call as I thought Pierre had already contacted a search firm on your behalf. The firm you used to recruit Margot identified an excellent candidate."

"No, we haven't started our search. Pierre said you supported his interim management of our audit function until the pandemic restrictions are lifted and the full committee can conduct face-to-face interviews with potential candidates."

I consider my response. "Yes, I agreed he could provide interim oversight, but thought your

---

committee should proceed with your search. We must have had a misunderstanding. Do you want me to call him?"

"Not necessary, I will tell him the committee is contacting the firm we used to find Margot."

#   #   #

It's wonderful to be back on Paradox, but I miss being with Amanda, and we talk every night. This weekend's weather is ideal for moving Paradox to Boothbay Harbor on Sunday, so we skip our weekend visit. Saturday night, she asks about my social media project.

"Almost done. It's been a process of elimination, and Logan's friends post something new every day. Logan has fifteen social media friends who work at investment banks and only one is involved with these mergers. None of Logan's friends work for any companies or law firms involved with any of these transactions."

"Logan's older sister, Ashley, worked at a restaurant frequented by lawyers and investment bankers before the lockdown. She was the hostess and posted selfies on her accounts with people at the restaurant."

"Ashley has hundreds of friends who are not friends of her brother. I've isolated over a hundred photos she's posted with investment bankers, financial analysts, and corporate lawyers at the restaurant. I've identified Noah, Logan's friend, with Ashley in dozens of photos."

"A girl named Savannah is another friend of

Ashley's. What's most interesting, these two young women both posted photos of people celebrating successful financial transactions at the restaurant. The dates for thirteen celebrations match merger announcements for Logan's investments. The party for the fourteenth celebration was canceled when the lockdown was announced."

"Noah and Ashley both posted photos of themselves sharing affectionate embraces at merger celebrations matching three of Logan's investments. Ashley posted a photo of an investment banker named Jacob hugging her at celebrations related to four of Logan's investments. Both Savannah and Ashley posted photos of Savannah kissing and holding hands with a lawyer named Richard at celebrations matching six of Logan's trades. The last party with Richard's firm was canceled."

"I believe these two young women are the key to Logan's insider investments, and the lockdown disrupted their social life. Ashley is still in New York, but the restaurant is closed and Savannah returned to Atlanta. I've told my client my analysis will be completed next week."

"The wind and seas should be calm tomorrow, and I plan to depart early for Boothbay Harbor."

23

Boothbay Harbor/Aboard Paradox

Kim waves from the dock as I approach Boothbay Harbor Marina Sunday afternoon. "Welcome back! How was your voyage?"

I toss Kim my lines. "Foggy after I passed Owls Head Light. My radar helped avoid the lobster boats pulling traps, but dodging their buoys was an adventure."

Paradox arrives at her summer home

I text a photo and message to Amanda;

Arrived safely – seas calm but a foggy voyage. It was marvelous to be underway again.

#   #   #

Amanda calls Sunday night, "How's Boothbay?"

"I'm happy to be back, delivered signed books to Sherman's bookstore and explored the waterfront this evening. Kim says Lincoln County only has a few Covid cases and they want to keep it that way. The Harbor Master even included a handmade fabric facemask in my welcome bag."

"Like Belfast, facemasks are mandatory when entering any shop or art gallery and, most people wear their facemasks outside. The marinas are open, but several hotels and restaurants are not opening this summer. Restaurants with outside seating are open, there is a food truck near the walking bridge and Dan's Red Cup Coffeehouse offers sidewalk service for my morning latte. It's encouraging to see most of the shops adjusting to the situation and ready to operate safely for this summer's tourist season."

I ask, "How was your weekend?"

"Good. It was warm in Portland, and I met two of my girlfriends for a walk along the waterfront. We had takeout from a Thai restaurant for lunch. I need to find more time to visit with my friends."

#   #   #

Pierre calls Monday morning, "Monsieur Wilson, I understand you had a call with Monsieur Hedinger to discuss the search for Louis's successor."

"Yes, he called me last week, and I agree it's time for the committee to initiate their search."

He replies, "Good, I'm ready to end this time-consuming burden. The committee has hired the same firm they used to recruit Margot. I also welcome any suggestions you might have and will make certain the committee considers them. The members of the committee respect your opinion."

"Thank you, I'm happy to offer my opinion if I'm acquainted with the candidate but, you are correct, these Covid restrictions make it awkward to evaluate potential candidates."

Pierre says, "Yes, times are difficult. I am now working from an old family villa in Switzerland I inherited a few years ago. Having a little more space and a view of Lake Geneva is more inviting than my apartment in Paris. How about you? I think it must be depressing to be in New York."

"Thanks for asking. I moved to an apartment in Maine when New York was locked down in March. I'm currently on my boat."

"Is this the boat you describe in your books? Where are you now and, with Covid restrictions, how much freedom to move about do you have?"

"Yes, Paradox is the name for my boat. I'm in Boothbay Harbor and plan to make it my summer base as it's closer to Portland. My only cruising will be along the coast of Maine due to Covid travel restrictions. We are both very fortunate - many people are out of work and confined to home."

Pierre sighs, "Yes, we are very fortunate."

#   #   #

Wednesday afternoon, I email my client in Denver.

I've completed my investigation and have attached my report. In summary, I believe Ashley, Logan's sister, is the source of his insider tips. As I describe, Ashley and Savannah, one of Ashley's girlfriends, both had relationships with men with access to insider information.

Let's schedule a time Friday afternoon to discuss my findings. The next step will be for you to share my report with securities regulators and the FBI. I believe my analysis will provide the roadmap required to open an official investigation.

# # #

Amanda arrives Friday evening and says, "I missed you last week. The apartment seems empty when I get home from work." We share a long embrace and kiss.

We put her canvas duffel and leather backpack in the stateroom, and I offer her a glass of Cabernet Sauvignon. "I'm grilling beef tenderloin tonight."

She says, "Great, I'm starving. How was your call with Denver today?"

"They reviewed my report with their attorneys and are submitting it to securities regulators and the FBI next week."

I continue, "I have mixed feelings at this stage of an investigation. I help clients isolate and report suspicious activity and close accounts. Securities regulators and the FBI decide if further action is warranted. Without charges, the schemers can just relocate and start again."

Amanda smiles, "Mark says your reports provide the best roadmaps for his investigators. You make it easy for them to follow fraudulent activity and prosecute a case."

# # #

I wake to the aroma of brewing coffee at daybreak Saturday morning and say, "Why are you up at five o'clock?"

"It's a beautiful morning and I'm happy to be back aboard Paradox. We've been cooped up in my apartment for the past three months. Let's enjoy our newfound freedom, these longer days, warmer weather, and take a dinghy ride around the harbor after breakfast."

Boothbay Harbor Public Landing

Mid-afternoon, Amanda says "Hi" to Dan and orders cappuccinos from him at the Red Cup's walk-up window. We cross the street to enjoy them at a picnic table overlooking Boothbay Harbor's public landing.

Saturday night, we buy takeout lobster rolls with sweet potato fries and return to the boat for dinner with a glass of Chardonnay. After dinner, we hold hands and view a red sunset from the aft deck. We share an affectionate kiss and I whisper, "Your blue eyes sparkle when you're happy."

"I'm happy to be with you."

#   #   #

Sunday afternoon, I buy our afternoon lattes at the Red Cup and we find an empty picnic table at the public landing. Amanda smiles and reaches for my hand, "What a wonderful weekend. It's refreshing to be back aboard Paradox and enjoy the sunshine and warmer weather. It almost feels normal when I close my eyes."

## 24

Boothbay Harbor/Aboard Paradox

The summer sun rises early in Downeast Maine, and Amanda starts back to Portland at five o'clock Monday morning. I spend the next two days on routine calls with my banking clients.

I'm riding my bike to Hannaford's on Wednesday morning when I hear a car hit the curb behind me. My handlebars jerk as I glance over my shoulder and I'm headed face first into the concrete.

"Are you OK?"

I'm disoriented, it's unclear who is standing over me and I slowly answer, "I think so. What happened?"

"Looks like you hit a rut and took a nasty fall."

I move my hand to my forehead, "I'm bleeding. Is it bad?"

"It doesn't look good. Do you think anything is broken?"

As my vision clears, I see an older woman asking me questions. I struggle to sit and ask, "Were you driving the car?"

"What car? I was coming up the hill from Hannaford's and stopped when I saw you face down on the sidewalk. You don't look good. I've called 911 and our emergency service is on its way."

# # #

Time is a blur as I'm rolled onto a stretcher, driven to the emergency room, and examined under a bright light. A woman's voice behind a medical mask says, "Mr. Wilson, I'm concerned you may have a concussion and we want to keep you overnight for observation."

I'm too dazed to object, "OK."

# # #

"Good morning, how do you feel?"

I open my eyes, "Not sure, where am I?"

"We kept you overnight for observation, do you remember?"

I glance around, "Yes. You're the voice behind the mask. I'm feeling better than yesterday."

"Good. I want to run a few more tests, but you can probably go back to your boat later today."

"How do you know I'm on a boat?"

She laughs, "This is a small town. Your driver's license and a boat card were in your jeans. An empty Harbor Master's welcome bag was with your bike. Jeff said you were at Kim's marina."

#   #   #

I'm discharged Thursday noon and, to my surprise, Amanda greets me with a gentle kiss at the door.

I try to smile, "The doctor said Kim was providing transportation, thanks for coming."

Amanda says, "Kim called me yesterday, and she recovered your bike. I drove down last night. They aren't letting any visitors in the medical center because of Covid, so I had to wait on Paradox until you were discharged."

"I should have called, but I didn't want to worry you."

She smiles, "No broken bones or concussion, you were lucky. Your bike needs a new front wheel."

"Sorry, I don't feel lucky with these bandages wrapped around my head, face, and arms. The doctor gave me a prescription for pain medication and I'm going to need it."

"What happened, what did you hit?"

"I remember glancing back when I heard a car hit the curb behind me. It's a blur after that."

"What happened to the car?"

"I don't know."

"Let's get you back to Paradox and into bed."

#   #   #

Amanda fixes me a bowl of chicken noodle soup for dinner and I recover enough to grin. "I thought soup was my specialty."

My cell phone rings before Amanda can offer a sarcastic reply and she says, "You have a call from 'Rembrandt'."

"Thanks, I'll take it." I answer, "Sarah?"

"Yes, how are you? Sounds like you had a nasty bike accident."

"I'm recovering. How did you know?"

She laughs, "You pay me to monitor your online presence, just doing my job. The emergency service logged your accident in their system and it flagged an alert on my software."

"Do I want to know how you do that?"

"No. So, how are you?"

"Like I said, recovering. Amanda came from Portland and is playing nurse."

"Good, I just wanted to check. I've seen your name pop up on the dark web, but I can't read the encrypted messages. You've attracted somebody's attention again. What happened?"

"I glanced back when I heard a car hit the curb. I remember seeing a car behind me before I lost control and fell. The driver didn't stop to help me."

Sarah hesitates, "The driver didn't stop? That's strange. Take care and say hello to Amanda."

———

111

"Thanks, I appreciate your call."

Amanda looks pensive, "Why didn't you tell me the car was heading your direction?"

"Sorry, I'm just beginning to remember what happened."

25

Boothbay Harbor/Aboard Paradox

I'm still half-asleep when I hear Amanda's voice, "Are you hungry?"

"Wow – What time is it? How long did I sleep?"

"The pain medication you took after dinner knocked you out last night – it's almost noon on Friday. Want some coffee and breakfast?"

"That sounds good – thanks."

#   #   #

Amanda drives me to the medical center Saturday morning for a check-up and bandage change. We both wait in the parking lot until they process my Covid test.

I return an hour later, "Can you play nurse next week? The doctor gave me this package of medication, gauze, and medical tape to use every day and she wants to see me again next Wednesday."

"What did she say?"

"No concussion, no infection, and take the pain

medication every six hours, if needed."

I pause and hold her hand. "I'm glad you're here. How long can you stay?"

"I called Mark. He said no problem – it doesn't make any difference where I work, so long as the job gets done."

"Wonderful. I'll need help with these bandages and happy you can play nurse."

Amanda says, "I'm disappointed the Lobster Boat Races and Windjammer Days were canceled because of Covid. These events are the traditional kick-off to summer in the Boothbay region and would have been fun this week."

# # #

Monday morning, Amanda takes her cup of coffee to the settee table and opens her laptop. She says, "This gives me enough space to work for short periods of time. The boat's network connections provide both of us with secure online and voice communication."

Paradox doesn't provide privacy for Amanda's conference call on Monday afternoon. I'm feeling better, buy a latte at the Red Cup, and walk to a picnic table at the public landing.

When I return, she says, "Sorry. I hate to kick you off your boat, but I can't do a classified video call from a public picnic table."

"Don't worry, it's a small price to pay for such a beautiful nurse. I'm glad you can stay."

\#   \#   \#

To my surprise, Sebastian Hedinger, Chair of the Paris bank's audit committee, calls me on Wednesday, "Monsieur Wilson, we have an interesting candidate and I wish to ask your opinion. Do you recall Johanna Schmidt?"

"Please, call me Steve. Johanna managed the bank's audit program in Japan for me. Has she inquired about the bank's position?"

"Yes, Ms. Schmidt is interested in returning to Europe and responded to an inquiry from the search firm. What are your thoughts?"

"I don't recruit employees from my former bank; however, I can offer my opinion if she responded to the search firm. Johanna is a wonderful choice. She and Margot were two of my top performers."

"Excellent. Her credentials are superb and I will make her an offer today."

Amanda is using her laptop on the settee table and says, "Can I ask about Johanna?"

"Sure. She worked for Margot in Europe. Like many Europeans, she speaks multiple languages and she accepted a promotion as manager of our audit function in Japan. She's interested in returning to Europe and inquired about the Paris opportunity."

\#   \#   \#

Two days later, I receive an email from Johanna:

Sebastian Hedinger told me you are an advisor to

the Paris bank's audit committee. I look forward to working with you again. I accepted the bank's offer this morning and have given my notice. I have an excellent staff and my Japanese assistant is being promoted. I will move and start my new position in Paris at the end of July.

I reply:

Congratulations - Great news! The Paris bank is lucky to have you as their new Chief Auditor. My official role is limited to a single investigation, but I am always available for discussions with you.

#   #   #

An hour later, I receive a call from Pierre. "Monsieur Hedinger just told me Johanna Schmidt has accepted our offer. This is excellent news and I want you to be the first to know. I've read her profile and I'm impressed by her international experience. If I'm correct, she worked for Margot in Europe before moving to Japan."

"Yes, Johanna is the same caliber as Margot. The audit committee has made an excellent decision."

Pierre says, "I must arrange to meet her in Paris and brief her on the status of our investigations. The audit committee prepared an announcement about her selection for me to share with the audit staff today and all bank employees tomorrow. It will be a relief to transfer this responsibility to Ms. Schmidt. I hope international Covid restrictions don't interfere with her arrival."

26

July - Boothbay Harbor/Aboard Paradox

Saturday morning, Amanda says, "I'm glad to see the doctor provided smaller bandages, you're beginning to look normal again."

"Thanks, you've been a wonderful nurse. The pain is almost gone and I'm beginning to feel normal again. I can't work feeling groggy and stopped taking those damn pain pills two days ago."

"My nurse excuse is ending, and it's awkward for both of us to work full time from Paradox. It's time for me to return to Portland after we celebrate the 4th of July this coming Friday."

I ask, "What would you like to do for the holiday weekend?"

"Nothing. This will be a short work week, and I expect people from Portland will be taking advantage of the summer weather for the three-day weekend. The Governor announced people from nearby states with low Covid counts can visit Maine without a two-week quarantine. I expect it to be busy and I want to stay away from crowds."

She continues, "We both have work to do the next few days, and then let's celebrate being together. I plan to drive back Sunday morning to avoid post-holiday traffic."

"I'll miss you, but I won't be getting up at the crack of dawn next week."

#   #   #

"Steve, what's wrong? Why are you out on the aft deck in the middle of the night?"

"I had a bad dream and can't get back to sleep."

"You never have trouble sleeping – tell me about your dream."

"It was about my accident. I'm looking back and see the car headed at me. The driver is a woman with dark hair wearing a fedora. I woke up in a cold sweat. I got up to look at the security video when I couldn't go back to sleep."

"Security video?"

"The woman in my dream reminded me of the woman leaving Margot's apartment building."

"What do you mean?"

"The doctor was right – hitting my head affected my memory of the accident. I remember more every day. The woman driving the car in my dream had long dark hair, sunglasses, a facemask, and she was wearing a black fedora."

I continue, "The witness to Louis's accident said the driver was a woman with long dark hair wearing a large hat with a facemask. Is it a coincidence a woman with a similar description was at all three locations? That's why I can't sleep."

I pause, "Margot must have had something on that laptop that got her killed. Louis must have uncovered the secret. Why me? What's the connection?"

Amanda massages my shoulder, "Steve, it's the middle of Saturday night and you've had a bad dream. Lots of women with dark hair wear large hats."

"Let's go back to bed and talk in the morning."

#   #   #

I wake to the aroma of coffee and a smile from Amanda. "Good morning. A little sunshine and coffee always help me forget a bad dream."

"Thanks. In this case, it brings clarity. It wasn't just a dream. I was remembering my accident. I think it will help if we walk up to the road. There's no place to park and the exercise will be beneficial."

"OK. Enjoy your coffee and get dressed."

#   #   #

An hour later. "Let's see, I was about halfway down the hill. Yes, do you see this tire mark on the curb and up into grass?"

I walk a few more steps. "These tire marks show where the car returned to the road."

"This rough sidewalk section must be where I lost control. These dark stains look like blood and show where I landed. I remember the bike twisting to the right and heading face down onto the concrete. I didn't dive straight down onto the sidewalk. I fell to the right and landed on this driveway."

"The driver would have hit this power pole if they tried to follow me. My accident threw me out of the car's path. What do you think?"

Scene of Steve's Bicycle Accident

Amanda's skeptical, "First, we can't prove the tire tracks happened at the same time as your accident. Second, both countries are in lockdown. How would this woman travel from France to Maine? Third, lots of women have dark hair and wear sun hats."

"OK, good points. Let's walk back to the Red Cup for a latte and find an empty picnic table at the public landing."

#   #   #

I smile after buying our lattes. "A toast, thanks for

taking good care of me and listening to my accident theory."

Amanda's pensive. "Are you certain the driver had dark hair and was wearing a fedora?"

"Last night wasn't just a bad dream. The pain medication combined with hitting my head on the concrete didn't help my memory, but I remember what happened. When I glanced over my shoulder, I saw a woman with dark hair wearing a hat and a facemask. I'm not sure it was a black fedora. It's probably a coincidence."

Amanda says, "I'm skeptical, but it's surprising to me the driver didn't stop. What if it's not a coincidence? What if Margot and Louis were about to uncover something incriminating?"

"Why me?"

She smiles, "This wouldn't be the first time your curiosity resulted in a hospital visit. You keep asking questions about Margot's death. If you're correct about a connection, then you need to warn Pierre and Johanna."

27

Boothbay Harbor/Aboard Paradox

Monday dawns sunny with the aroma of fresh coffee. I yawn, "Why are you getting me up at five o'clock?"

"I enjoy these bright mornings after a long dreary winter with short days. Here's your coffee. Europe is six hours ahead of Maine and you need to make your calls. I'll take my coffee and laptop outside to Kim's picnic table on the dock. Let me know when you finish and we can have breakfast."

#   #   #

"Bonjour Monsieur Hedinger, sorry to bother you. I have a concern I wish to discuss."

"Please, call me anytime. What is your concern?"

"I don't want to sound like an alarmist, but I think it pays to be careful. The bank has lost two Chief Auditors this year under suspicious circumstances."

"Yes, it is worrisome. I was delighted when Margot accepted the position when our Chief Auditor retired. I wasn't certain Louis was up to the job. Thankfully, he proved to be an excellent choice."

"What is your concern?"

"I am concerned about Johanna's safety. A car almost hit me under suspicious circumstances last Wednesday. A woman with dark hair wearing a black hat was driving the car. This is the same description for the unidentified woman leaving the service door at Margot's apartment and the driver of the auto that killed Louis. I don't like three coincidences."

The phone is silent for a moment. "Are you certain about the driver of the car that almost hit you?"

"Yes, she was wearing a facemask, so I can't describe her in more detail."

"What do you want me to do?"

"Nothing. I plan to call Pierre and send an email to Johanna to alert them to the possibility these three events are related. They both need to be extra careful."

"I agree, thanks for the call. Let me know if the audit committee needs to take any action."

# # #

"Bonjour Pierre, sorry to bother you. I have a concern I wish to discuss."

"Please, call anytime."

"I don't want to sound like an alarmist, but I think it pays to be careful. I was almost hit by a car driven by a woman with dark hair wearing a fedora last Wednesday."

"Were you injured?"

"Not seriously, but I'm concerned about your safety if my accident is related to the deaths of Margot and Louis. I don't like coincidences."

"Monsieur Wilson, you are being melodramatic. The police have investigated both of their deaths."

"I just want to alert you to the possibility you might be in danger if their deaths and my accident are related to an investigation at the bank. I think it's prudent if you take extra precautions."

"I feel perfectly safe. Both my Paris apartment and this villa have security systems. I hope you don't plan to contact Ms. Schmidt. We don't want to frighten her before she starts her new position."

"I'll be sensitive, but I want to alert her to the possibility."

#   #   #

Johanna's in Japan, so I email a note asking her to call me. Tokyo is thirteen hours ahead of Boothbay and my phone rings at ten o'clock Monday evening.

Johanna says, "Hello, I saw your note in my morning email."

"Thanks for calling. Sorry to bother you before you start your new position, but I have a concern I wish to discuss."

"Is it about Margot and Louis?"

"Yes, why do you ask?"

"I did my research before inquiring about this position. Taking a position where my predecessors both died under suspicious circumstances was troublesome. I didn't know you were working with the bank until Sebastian Hedinger offered me the position. I accepted based on your relationship."

"The bank has not retained me. I volunteered to investigate the circumstances related to Margot's death. Pierre and Sebastian asked my opinion about promoting Louis, and Sebastian asked my opinion of you. My relationship with the bank remains informal."

"Interesting, not quite the way Hedinger explained your relationship to me – why did you call?"

"There might be a connection between their deaths and I want you to be careful."

#   #   #

Amanda asks, "How were your calls with the bank in Paris?"

"I alerted Monsieur Hedinger, Pierre, and Johanna to the possibility the events are related and advised them to be extra careful. The calls with Hedinger and Pierre were short. It's hard to read Hedinger, he is very formal and inscrutable. Pierre remains skeptical."

I pause, "Johanna and I had a long call. She asked a lot of questions."

#   #   #

Mark calls Amanda later in the week. I put on my

facemask and take my laptop to Kim's picnic table on the dock to give them privacy.

Amanda is smiling when she waves me back to the boat. "Mark added your Denver investigation to my assignments. He said it's the most efficient way to manage the case. He sent a copy of your report to me and my job is to manage the investigation with our agents in Denver, New York, and Atlanta. Mark said he told your client in Denver they are not the subject of the investigation and he received their consent for you to consult with the FBI. Let's talk after I read your full report."

#   #   #

The next morning, we discuss the case with lattes from Red Cup on the back deck. She says, "It's nice to share ideas on a case again. Your report's what I expected, so have you considered a plan of action?"

I answer, "It's a complex case involving six suspects. The diagram in my report illustrates the connections and flow of inside information for each merger to Logan."

"My analysis starts with Logan and his sister Ashley. Logan and his sister are both friends with Noah, a junior analyst at an investment bank involved in three of the mergers. Noah also has social media accounts, and he and Ashley post photos of themselves together at celebrations for the transactions. Noah is single and they both post frequent photos together at other parties."

"Ashley's social media pages also link her to Jacob, an older investment banker who worked on four of these mergers. Jacob doesn't use social media, but Ashley has posted photos of them hugging and holding hands at celebrations for four of these mergers. Jacob's profile page on the investment firm's website includes his photo, and he holds a senior position in the merger department. Additional research shows Jacob lives with his wife and two children in New Jersey."

Denver Insider Trading Analysis				
		Logan		
		^		
		14 Mergers		
		^		
> > > > > > > > >		Ashley	< < < < <	Savannah
^		^		^
3 Mergers		4 Mergers		7 Mergers
^		^		^
Noah		Jacob		Richard

"Finally, we have social media posts from Ashley's friend, Savannah, showing her with Richard, an older attorney who's worked on seven of these mergers. Richard doesn't use social media, and Savanah only posted his first name. However, the law firm's website includes his photo and says he is a senior partner in their merger section. I suspect Richard doesn't know compromising photos of them together are posted on the internet. My research confirms Richard is married and lives with his wife in Connecticut."

"I've never encountered a complex insider trading case with three separate sources of inside information, and it took me four months to identify the connections. We only have Logan's suspicious trades as evidence. A successful prosecution will require tracing his inside information back to the three insiders."

Amanda says, "We need to find a weak link. Your report should provide sufficient evidence to obtain a search warrant for relevant phone, email, text, and computer records for Logan and his sister, Ashley. Once we start, I want to keep the pressure on Logan, Ashley, and Savannah. Their testimony is essential to convict Noah, Jacob, and Richard."

I smile, "I'm glad Mark assigned the investigation to you. It gives me an opportunity to follow-up and help solve the case."

#   #   #

We put on our facemasks and help Kim with lines as boats arrive Thursday afternoon for the 4th of July holiday weekend. Amanda was right. She and Kim are busy greeting friends arriving on their boats from Portland.

Thursday evening is awkward. Boaters are a friendly group and normally shake hands, share hugs, and gossip with old friends. This year is different with facemasks and social distancing. I'm impressed - everyone adjusts and we all manage to accommodate the new safety protocols.

Amanda prepares dinner aboard the boat and says, "We will see more boats from Portland cruising Downeast this year with the Covid restrictions. Both Canada and The Bahamas have closed their borders, and it's safer for our friends to stay in Maine than cruise along the east coast."

28

Boothbay Harbor/Aboard Paradox

I'm alone when I wake up Monday morning and miss the aroma of fresh coffee. The marina was busy over the holiday, but the weekend visitors headed home late Sunday.

Boothbay Harbor is quiet as I walk up to the Red Cup to buy my morning coffee at Dan's sidewalk carryout window. Mark calls just as I return to Paradox and get comfortable at my desk.

"Good morning. Thanks for agreeing to consult with Amanda on the Denver investigation."

He pauses, "How are you feeling?"

"Much better, Amanda is an outstanding nurse."

"Good, she told me you had a nasty bike accident."

"I don't think it was an accident. I'm worried my bike accident is connected to the deaths of both Margot and Louis. It must have something to do with an investigation, and I still suspect it's related to Margot's visit to New York."

I continue, "The Paris bank recruited Johanna as their new Chief Auditor and we discussed Margot's investigation last week. I'm convinced we are overlooking some clues."

Mark is skeptical. "We closed that case. We traced the money from Margot's investigation and shut down the operation. Treasury has sanctioned the people involved. What more could be relevant?"

"I don't know. Is it OK with you if I keep Amanda informed?"

"Sure, her involvement will be unofficial, but if something develops, we can always reopen our investigation."

#   #   #

Amanda calls Monday afternoon to update me on her Denver investigation. "Our attorneys presented our case to a judge this morning. She granted the search warrant for Logan's electronic records, including his computer, email, text, and phone records. Our search warrant was delivered to Logan this afternoon."

"The judge said we had insufficient evidence to request a search warrant for his sister's records. She wants more evidence linking Ashley to Logan's securities transactions before she approves our request for her records."

Amanda sends me a text Wednesday morning:

Logan retained one of Ashley's New York friends as his attorney. We've scheduled a video conference with Logan and his attorney tomorrow to discuss the delivery of his electronic records.

Thursday night, I ask, "How was your conference call with Logan and his attorney? I've never talked with him and have no idea how he might respond."

"Logan didn't say much, his young attorney did her best to control the interview. Logan claims he searches online for merger rumors and invests on his hunches."

"They agreed to provide access to all the records requested by our warrant, but Logan said we shouldn't expect many files. He said he deletes all email and text messages after they are read. I reminded his attorney our warrant requires access to cloud accounts, trash, and backup files. I told her I expect to get all of Logan's records on Monday."

#   #   #

Amanda arrives at the marina Friday evening in time for me to prepare swordfish on the grill. She prepares a salad and I move the settee table to the aft deck. After dinner, we enjoy a Grand Marnier while admiring the full moon and stars in a cloudless night sky.

#   #   #

Our weekend plans include cruising a short distance to pick up a mooring at Christmas Cove. The stars and moon shine bright in the clear night sky as we sip wine on the aft deck Saturday night.

Sunday morning, Amanda snuggles close, "I'm glad we've returned to our pre-pandemic pattern of working separately during the week and relaxing together on weekends. It was stressful for me

———

131

trying to balance work and play while you were working at my apartment."

"I agree, it's best when we reserve weekends for boating adventures. How about another overnight cruise when you come back next weekend?"

"Lovely idea."

Amanda prepares a lobster casserole and we stream a movie after dinner Sunday evening. Before departing at daybreak Monday morning, she says, "What a nice weekend. We finally found time to unwind. Your accident delayed plans for our weekend cruise and I've been swamped with my new job. We need to do a better job of planning. Maine summers are short."

29

Boothbay Harbor/Aboard Paradox

I'm juggling a variety of assignments for my banking clients, but Amanda's Denver investigation consumes my attention this week. It's a relief we can work together on Logan's case and she calls me Monday afternoon.

"Logan's attorney provided his phone records, email, and text messages this morning. Her attachments show he deleted his messages the day a deputy sheriff served our search warrant. They were recovered from his backup account. Your password for access is attached."

I call Amanda Monday evening. "I've searched all his messages for reference to merger transactions. The only hits are related to his investment account. I found no incriminating messages."

Amanda says, "The only pattern I see is phone calls with his sister before he makes every investment. If Ashley's the source, then all their inside information is shared verbally."

I add, "Logan receives emails from several stock market newsletters. I'll search the newsletter sites tomorrow to see if they mention possible mergers before he purchases stock."

#   #   #

I'm smiling when I call Amanda Tuesday morning, "Logan made a mistake. I finished reviewing his text messages last night and discovered a text to Ashley with a stock symbol followed by a question mark. He had two letters in the stock symbol reversed. She replied, *'RK!'*, the correct order for two of the stock symbol's four letters. The trade confirmation shows he purchased the shares a few minutes later. This text confirms Ashley is Logan's source."

#   #   #

Tuesday afternoon, I send a text to Amanda:

I broke their code!

Logan sends a text message to Ashley after he sells his shares and deposits the profits in his money market account:

He says: Financial aid deposited. Thanks!

She replies: Great - more to come.

These text messages should be sufficient to obtain a search warrant to examine Ashley's phone, computer, and investment accounts.

Thursday evening, Amanda calls, "Our search warrant was served late yesterday and Ashley is being represented by the same attorney as her brother. Ashley's attorney is calling me tomorrow to discuss the warrant."

#   #   #

Amanda's beaming when she arrives Friday night and we walk across the footbridge for dinner on the deck at Coastal Prime. We are seated at an outside table with a spectacular view of the harbor and we both order a glass of Chardonnay.

Amanda proposes our evening toast, "To Logan's mistake and Ashley's financial aid. Ashley's attorney must have explained the penalty for destruction of evidence, and she called me to say I will receive Ashley's records on Monday."

"Good, now let's agree to ignore business for the rest of the weekend and find a nearby cove to anchor out Saturday night."

30

Boothbay Harbor/Aboard Paradox

Amanda departs for Portland at daybreak on Monday. I take my morning walk, buy a latte at Red Cup, and return to Paradox to review Ashley's social media accounts. I'm amused - she has removed all photos of the merger celebrations. I say to myself, "Too late, I copied and included each of those photos with my report."

I check Savannah's accounts and see she has not deleted her romantic comments and photos with the married lawyer.

The balance of my day is devoted to email and video calls with my banking clients.

#   #   #

Amanda calls Tuesday morning, "I received Ashley's electronic records an hour ago. As I suspected, the messages are all copies from her computer's backup files and the dates show she deleted email and text messages the day our search warrant was served to her brother. I've sent you a link."

Amanda continues, "Ashley's brokerage statements are a surprise. She is an active trader and buys or sells stocks every few days."

I reply, "That is a surprise. I will start my analysis by reviewing her investment account."

#   #   #

Ashley's investment account shows the same successful merger investments as Logan. She and her brother have benefited from the same insider information. Ashley's other investments show a mix of gains and losses, mostly losses.

I email my discovery to Amanda:

Ashley made her first merger related trade based on information from Savannah. Richard worked on the transaction and Savannah sent the following text to Ashley the week before they announced this transaction.

We need to plan a party next week when Richard's merger is announced!

Amanda calls me, "Savannah's text message combined with her social media photos is enough to request our search warrant for her records."

I respond, "Is Savannah our next target?"

Amanda says, "No, why don't we contact her married boyfriend next? I haven't mentioned our suspicions about Savannah to Ashley's attorney, and contacting Richard should be a surprise. I don't expect to find any evidence he was engaged in insider trading – our best argument is he traded information for a sexual relationship."

She continues, "I suggest you call Richard and tell him you've been hired by a brokerage firm to investigate a series of suspicious trades related to a merger his firm negotiated. You want to ask him a few questions to confirm the timeline of events."

I smile, "I like the idea of asking Richard for his cooperation and will do my best to set up a video call with him."

31

Virtual Interview with Richard

Thursday – July 23, 2020

"Good afternoon, Richard. Thanks for responding to my email. As I explained, I have been retained by a brokerage firm to investigate suspicious trades by a college student in Denver. I appreciate your cooperation and our video call will let me share a few documents on the screen with you."

Q: "First, I have posted the timeline of events on our computer screens. It may be circumstantial, but he made this first trade prior to the public announcement of the merger. This transaction was negotiated by your firm, and I'm trying to establish the timeline of events. His trade occurred a year ago and the image on our screens highlights the date of his investment, the date of the merger announcement, and the date he sold the shares. I'm sure, from this timeline, you can see why his trade looks suspicious. This student purchased the shares ten days before your public announcement and sold them for a nice profit the day after the announcement. Are you aware of any pre-merger news that might have influenced his purchase?"

A: "No, we are very careful about confidentiality and I don't recall any significant price moves prior to any of our recent transactions."

Q: "You are correct. This merger transaction wasn't preceded by any significant price movement. I have located no pre-announcement rumors or publicity. However, I have traced information relating to his trade back to an individual you might know. Do you recognize anyone in this picture?"

A: "Of course, that's me with a group of people."

Q: "You are standing next to a young woman. Do you recognize her?"

A: He hesitates, "She looks familiar."

Q: "Her name is Savannah, and she's posted pictures of the two of you on her social media pages. Does that help refresh your memory?"

A: "As I recall, she attended several of our merger celebrations. It looks like the photo of this group was taken at a restaurant."

Q: "That's correct. How would you describe your relationship with Savannah?"

A: He pauses, "I don't see how this is relevant. I probably talked to her at one of our celebrations."

Q: "I believe Savannah is the source of information for several of this student's pre-announcement trades. Do you have any idea how she might have known about these mergers before the public announcements?"

A: "No, I have no idea."

Q: "Is there any possibility she could have learned about them from anybody involved in negotiating the transactions?

A: "No, we all try to be very careful. Humm……. My team and I frequently go to that restaurant for dinner when we are working on deals. I suppose it's possible she eavesdropped on a conversation."

Q: "Just a few more questions. The list on your screen are additional trades made by this student before any public announcement of mergers which were negotiated by your firm. Please review this list with your team to see if they have ideas about pre-announcement leaks."

A: "Sure, we want to cooperate. I'm certain you will not find a connection and we want to protect the reputation of our firm."

Q: "Thank you. I have one more question. Please look at this social media post and photo. Why would Savannah think your relationship was personal?"

A: "This is nuts! This girl must be delusional. This conversation has ended."

#   #   #

An hour later, Amanda says, "Very interesting conversation. It's time to ask the judge for a search warrant of Savannah's records."

She continues, "I'll arrive in time for dinner tomorrow. Let's stay in Boothbay this weekend. We both need some downtime before you take Paradox to Belfast next week."

32

Belfast, Maine/Aboard Paradox

Monday morning, Amanda leaves Paradox at five o'clock for her drive back to Portland. I enjoy my morning walk and buy a latte and blueberry crumble at Red Cup. Kim helps me with the lines mid-morning and I depart for Front Street Shipyard in Belfast. The Eggemoggin Reach Regatta is next Saturday, and Amanda wants to arrive early to take photographs.

#   #   #

Tuesday morning, I receive a call from Johanna, "I loved Japan, but it's wonderful being back in Europe. I used an online service to rent a furnished apartment in a very secure building with a concierge. My Covid test was negative and yesterday was my first official day. I was pleased Chairman Richelieu called to welcome me to the bank. He was less formal than I expected and we had a cordial visit."

"I visited my new office for several hours. The entire audit staff and most other employees are working remotely, so the offices are mostly empty. Richelieu cares about staff safety and requested all non-essential employees work from home, so I plan to work from my new apartment."

"Have you visited with your new staff?"

"I called each member of the audit staff last week to introduce myself before I arrived in Paris. I've arranged to meet Pierre at an outdoor café tomorrow. He is working from his villa in Switzerland, but said he can return to Paris tonight for our lunch tomorrow."

She adds, "The management of this bank is very formal and my staff refers to Pierre as Monsieur Rochat. I report to the audit committee, so I plan to address him as Pierre. We always operated on a first-name basis."

I laugh, "Pierre acted aloof around the audit staff when I was in France. He prefers to call me Monsieur Wilson, but I address him as Pierre. The job of Chief Auditor is not subordinate to the bank's Chief Legal Counsel. However, I suspect Chairman Richelieu is still appropriate."

She continues, "I also called the head of security and the lawyers on Pierre's staff who work with audit to introduce myself. It's awkward meeting people during the pandemic, but my reception has been very cordial."

"Pierre arranged my passwords, so I have been able to review our active investigations. I also reviewed the year-end board and executive management audits while I was at the office. These reports provide unique insight into their backgrounds and financial activities."

"Richelieu is French and was elected Chairman ten years ago. He held senior positions at the bank's offices in Germany, Switzerland, Italy, and Spain before becoming Chairman. His family is one of the bank's largest shareholders."

"Sebastian Hedinger, Chair of our audit committee is Swiss. He is Chairman of a private investment management firm in Zurich. He joined the board ten years ago and was named Chair of the audit committee eight years ago. His disclosure form indicates some of his firm's clients own large stock positions in the bank. His form doesn't provide detailed information about his firm."

"The bank has board members from seven European countries and a diverse management team. Margot assembled an excellent staff, and Louis was doing a professional job as her successor. It's rare for a new manager to step into such a well-organized department. I'm reviewing my team's active investigations this week."

I reply, "Well done. I'm still concerned about a connection between Margot's death, her missing laptop, and Louis' death. Be careful, let's discuss anything suspicious you uncover. We need to keep you safe."

#   #   #

Amanda calls mid-week. "We provided the judge with Savannah's text message and her photos with Richard on Monday. The judge approved our search warrant, and Savannah is being represented by an attorney from Atlanta. He called me promptly and said they will cooperate and provide the required electronic documents early next week."

"I plan to leave early on Friday to arrive in Belfast in time for dinner. We want to get an early start on

Saturday for the Eggemoggin Reach Regatta."

# # #

Amanda wakes me at the crack of dawn on Saturday. I yawn, "The event doesn't start until eleven, we have plenty of time."

"It's a beautiful day for a spectacular event. I want to have time for a leisurely breakfast before we head down Eggemoggin Reach to Brooklin. We want to be there by ten to photograph the boats arriving."

Eggemoggin Reach Regatta

After breakfast, I untie our lines, and Amanda maneuvers Paradox out of her dock, through Belfast Harbor, and out into Penobscot Bay.

Amanda beams, "The Eggemoggin Reach Regatta is my favorite sailing event. The Brooklin Boat Yard started it thirty-five years ago with thirteen wooden boats. Over a hundred classic wooden sailboats typically take part, but Covid travel restrictions for boat owners reduced today's event to sixty-five yachts."

Amanda has a telescopic lens attached to her digital camera. I say, "I'll take the helm when we arrive at the starting line so you can take photos."

"Thanks. My Aunt Emma took me to my first regatta when I was a teenager. She hasn't missed a race and I hope to text her a photo of her lobster boat with the sailing fleet today."

#   #   #

We return to Belfast Saturday night and stroll the waterfront walkway to the food truck at the town park. Our dinner tonight is lobster rolls at a picnic table overlooking sailboats on their moorings in Belfast Harbor.

The sunset glows red on the horizon as we walk hand-in-hand back to the marina. I say, "We work well together, but our investigations intrude on our personal time. I'm glad we avoided discussing our investigations today."

Amanda stops to give me a kiss.

33

August - Belfast, Maine/Aboard Paradox

Amanda continues her routine of driving back to Portland at daybreak. Our return to weekend visits brings mixed emotions. I've lived alone for over thirty years and value my private time. Today, I miss Amanda during the week, look forward to our nightly phone calls and view each weekend with renewed anticipation.

#   #   #

Amanda calls Monday afternoon, "I received Savannah's materials an hour ago. She saved her email and text messages with Richard."

"Any sign Richard contacted Savannah after my interview with him."

She replies, "I see no recent text, email, or phone calls from Richard."

I say, "I'll review her investment account and messages this afternoon and we can talk later."

#   #   #

After dinner, I call Amanda. "Savannah's investment account has been inactive since she

---

returned to Atlanta. My analysis shows she opened her account with ten-thousand dollars and invested in seven merger transactions negotiated by Richard. She sold the shares after public announcements and withdrew her profits. She also purchased and sold shares in unrelated companies. She holds no investments today and her account still has ten-thousand in a money market account."

Amanda adds, "Her text messages with Richard reveal a very personal relationship and they arranged frequent rendezvous in her apartment. The fashion boutique where she worked closed with the Covid lockdown. She is unhappy Richard is working from home and can't leave to visit her apartment. She sent a text to Ashley saying she's bored living alone in New York and returned to her family in Atlanta."

I ask, "Does this give you sufficient information to request a search warrant for Richard's messages with Savannah – do you think it's worthwhile?"

"Not yet. I have my virtual interview with Savannah tomorrow and Ashley on Thursday. I want to know what they have to say about their relationships before taking any official action directed at Richard or the other insiders."

34

Virtual Interview with Savannah

Wednesday - August 5, 2020

"Savannah, thanks again for providing the electronic documents we requested and agreeing to this virtual interview with your attorney present. I want to remind you of your right to remain silent. Our video call is being recorded and your attorney has explained the importance of being truthful. Make certain you understand my question before you answer. We've already covered your background and preliminary information before our break. Next, I want to display a few documents for you to read."

Q: "Do you recognize this text message?"

We need to plan a party next week when Richard's merger is announced!

A: "Yes, I sent this to Ashley."

Q: "How did you know about this merger before the announcement?"

A: "My boyfriend, Richard, told me."

Q: "How did Richard know about the merger?"

A: "Richard's an important attorney and was working on the deal."

Q: "Was your relationship with Richard social or would you describe it as a personal relationship?"

A: Nervous laugh, "It was very personal."

Q: "Did you know your boyfriend was married?"

A: "Yes, but Richard is asking for a divorce."

Q: "Did you discuss marriage?"

A: "No, Richard said it was too early and he couldn't legally discuss marriage until his divorce was final."

Q: "When or where did Richard disclose this transaction?"

A: "I don't remember when, but it would have been at my apartment."

Q: "Did you ask him about this merger?"

A: "I didn't need to. He was always trying to impress me and bragging about how much money was involved in his deals."

Q: "Did Richard use drugs or drink excessively?"

A: "No, he was always careful in public and seldom had more than one drink before going to my apartment."

Q: "Did Richard use drugs or drink after you went to your apartment?"

A: Nervous giggle, "We would share a glass of Champagne after sex."

Q: "When was the last time you and Richard communicated?"

A: "He's working from home and said any communication could mess up his divorce. We haven't talked since the lockdown and I moved back to Atlanta."

Q: "Your brokerage account shows you purchased shares prior to seven mergers. How did you learn about all these transactions?"

A: "Richard told me I could make some money if I invested in these stocks."

Q: "Did you have a brokerage account before making these investments?"

A: "No, Richard told me how to open the account."

Q: "Where did you get the money to open your account? Did you have savings?"

A: Laughs, "You must be kidding – Richard gave me the money to open my account."

Q: "Did you make any other investments?"

A: "Yes, he told me to buy other stocks so my only investments weren't all big mergers."

Q: "Did you tell anyone about Richard's stock recommendations?"

A: "Yes, I told Ashley at the restaurant."

Q: "Why did you tell Ashley?"

A: "Just girl talk, but I told her she had to keep it to herself."

Q: "Did Ashley know you purchased these stocks?"

A: "Yes, I told her."

Q: "Did Ashley purchase any of these stocks?"

A: "No, I told her she couldn't."

Q: "Did Ashley share stock recommendations with you?"

A: "No, she knows nothing about stocks. She was just a hostess at the restaurant before it closed after the lockdown. I'm a pretty girl and she invited me to celebrate business deals with her customers. You know, free drinks and fancy meals. That's how I met Richard."

Q: "Let me share a document with you. This is a list of seven investments made by Ashley. Are these the stocks recommended by Richard?"

A: [checks document] "She wasn't supposed to buy these stocks!"

Q: "Next, I want to share a clip from a video interview with Richard."

[Savannah Watches Video]

A: "Bullshit, I can prove that SOB is lying."

35

Virtual Interview with Ashley

Thursday - August 6, 2020

"Ashley, thanks again for agreeing to this virtual interview. I want to remind you of your right to remain silent. Our video call is being recorded and your attorney has explained the importance of being truthful. Make certain you understand my question before you answer."

Q: "Where were you employed?"

A: "I'm on leave at a Wall Street restaurant and will return as the hostess when we are permitted to open for inside seating."

Q: "Were these photos from your social media account taken at the restaurant?"

A: "How did you get those? They aren't posted on my accounts."

Q: "Please answer my question. Were they taken at your restaurant?"

A: "Yes."

Q: "Your posts say these photos were taken at

celebrations. What were you celebrating?"

A: "I don't remember, we book a lot of parties at the restaurant."

Q: "These photos show the same people. Do you recognize Jacob, Noah, and Richard?"

A: "Yes, they are friends and frequently reserve a private room for parties to celebrate their deals."

Q: "Don't these celebrations represent merger announcements?"

A: "They might, I don't remember."

Q: "Did you own stock in any of these mergers?"

A: "I buy and sell stocks every week. I don't remember."

Q: "Let me refresh your memory. This document shows these photos match each date of thirteen merger announcements with stocks you owned in your brokerage account."

A: "I buy and sell stocks every week, sometimes I get lucky."

Q: "How did you know to buy each of these stocks weeks before any public announcement?"

A: "I might have overheard brokers talking at the restaurant. We are very popular with the Wall Street crowd. I don't remember."

Q: "Do you date Jacob?"

A: "Yes, we went out from time to time."

Q: "How would you describe your relationship?"

A: Laughs, "These older married guys are always good for an expensive dinner with a pretty girl."

Q: "You knew Jacob is married?"

A: "Sure, what of it?"

Q: "Did you know Jacob worked on the four mergers highlighted in yellow?"

A: "Maybe, I guess that's why he booked those celebrations."

Ashley's attorney: "Ashley, you shouldn't guess."

A: "OK, big deal."

Q: "Do you date Noah?"

A: "Noah's a friend of my brother. Yes, he's fun and we go out from time to time."

Q: "How would you describe your relationship with Noah?"

A: "He's not married and we can party late on weekends."

Q: "Did you know Noah worked on the three mergers highlighted in green?"

A: "If you say so, that's probably why he booked their celebrations at the restaurant."

Q: "Do you know why most of these celebrations were on a Monday night?"

A: "The guys told me they like to finish their work over the weekend so they can announce their deals before the markets open on Monday."

Q: "These photos suggest you attended all these celebrations - is that right?"

A: "Sure, I don't work Sunday and Monday nights, and the guys always want me at their parties."

Q: "Do you know Savannah?"

A: "Yes, she's a pretty girl who works during the day at a fashion boutique and likes to party at night. My customers like to have pretty girls at their parties."

Q: "Did you know she was dating Richard?"

A: "Sure, I think the guy's a creep. He was always hitting on me until I introduced him to Savannah. He loves her sweet southern accent."

Q: "This list highlights seven of your investments in orange. Do you recognize these stocks?"

A: "They look familiar."

Q: "Do you recall why you purchased these shares."

A: "No, I don't remember."

Q: "Did Savannah tell you about these stocks?"

A: "I doubt it, she knows nothing about investing."

Q: "Did you share your investment ideas with your brother?"

A: "He doesn't know anything about stocks, so sometimes I give him tips."

Q: "What kind of tips?"

A: "I don't know, just ideas."

Q: "Did you know he has a remarkable ability to invest in mergers before public announcements?"

A: Nervous laugh, "You must be kidding."

Q: "No, in fact, he has been investing in the same merger stocks as you. Were those your tips?"

A: "Maybe, I don't remember."

Q: "Do you refer to your tips as financial aid?"

A: "He can't afford graduate school, so maybe I made a few suggestions to help with expenses."

Q: "Do you know it's illegal to purchase stock in a merger based on non-public insider information?"

A: "Everybody does it, big deal."

## 36

Boothbay Harbor/Aboard Paradox

Amanda calls Friday morning, "I've been keeping our attorneys abreast of these developments. They agree we have sufficient evidence to request a search warrant for Richard next week."

"Savannah's social media account, messages and the transcript of her interview all link inside information flowing from Richard, to Savannah, to Ashley, to Logan. They believe we have sufficient evidence to file insider trading charges for Logan, Ashley, Savannah, and Richard."

"Savannah has been the most forthcoming and truthful person we interviewed. She is the direct link to Richard and our attorneys plan to offer her reduced charges for her testimony and complete cooperation."

"Filing charges will put pressure on Richard. He is the insider providing information for illegal trading by Savannah, Ashley, and Logan. They expect him to try to negotiate a deal."

"What about Noah and Jacob?"

"Ashley wasn't very forthcoming with incriminating testimony. We can match their transactions with celebrations at the restaurant, but that's not grounds for a conviction. We have sufficient evidence to charge Ashley with trading on inside information. We need to convince Ashley it's in her best interest to cooperate."

#   #   #

Amanda arrives Friday night and I grill chicken legs for dinner. "Your vacation starts in two weeks and I've confirmed our marinas. We will spend the last week of August visiting Rockland, Camden, and Castine in Penobscot Bay. We have a dock reserved at Northeast Harbor near Acadia National Park for the second week and return to Boothbay on Labor Day."

Amanda is smiling. "I can't wait, cruising Penobscot Bay is a delight and a week at Northeast Harbor sounds wonderful. I love the old carriage roads and walking the trails in Acadia. I know I'm fortunate, but my new job combined with the global pandemic and Maine's Covid restrictions has made this a stressful year. I'm looking forward to a work-free vacation."

## 37

Boothbay Harbor/Aboard Paradox

Johanna calls me on Monday, "I called Louis's wife over the weekend to express my sympathy. She told me Pierre stopped by after the accident to pick up Louis's work laptop and file folders on the desk. She surprised me by asking if I was comfortable stopping by to pick up some work-related papers she just discovered in the bedroom nightstand."

"I said sure and offered to buy her an afternoon coffee at a nearby outdoor café. She is very gracious and seemed to appreciate an opportunity to be outdoors. I didn't open the large envelope she handed me until I returned to my apartment."

"The envelope contains copies of several dozen documents and ten pages of handwritten notes. Louis was using his laptop to scan for wire transfer patterns similar to the Paris Connection. His notes suggest a connection between two other schemes and Margot's investigation. A question mark follows many of his notes. He made a note to 'discuss with Steve' on one of the wire transfers."

She pauses, "Louis planned to open two new case files, but was killed before he could do it. I've taken photos of the documents and his notes. I checked and your confidentiality agreement is still active. Is it OK if I email these photos to you?"

#   #   #

I call Johanna the following day. "These documents and Louis's notes confirm Margot's discovery is not an isolated matter. He uncovered two schemes to fund and influence politics in European countries. He didn't fully document his suspicions, and it's not clear from his notes if he discussed them with any of his staff or Pierre. What do you plan to do?"

She answers, "I plan to keep this between us for now. I need to finish examining these transactions and prepare my analysis."

#   #   #

My first call is to Amanda. "Johanna discovered additional evidence of money laundering. Louis was scanning wire transfers to determine if similar patterns were being used to disguise illegal political contributions. His notes indicate he uncovered two other schemes to influence politics in Europe."

"It's unclear if he discussed his suspicions with anyone, but he did plan to open two new files. I have copies of his notes and plan to check the status of each shell company involved."

She asks, "You're sure it's the same pattern used for the illegal transfers to our country?"

"Yes, just targeting European politics. I plan to update Mark tomorrow after I complete my analysis."

#   #   #

Wednesday, I call Mark. "Louis identified two other schemes similar to the Paris Connection. Neither involves domestic politics, so they are not within your jurisdiction. Is it OK for me to keep sharing information with Amanda?"

"Sure. Please keep me posted."

#　　#　　#

Johanna calls on Thursday. "I finished researching the accounts and the wire transfers to the fake organizations. No question, these funds are being used to make illegal political contributions and post fake news on social media accounts. I'm ready to present this to the audit committee at our meeting next week. I want to discuss it with Pierre and Sebastian Hedinger in advance. I've sent them a copy of my report and would appreciate you joining the conference call tomorrow morning."

#　　#　　#

Johanna's call with Pierre and Sebastian Hedinger starts at ten o'clock on Friday morning, so I'm up at three o'clock in the morning for our four o'clock conference call. Johanna looks very businesslike with her shoulder length dark hair and solid gray jacket on the video call. I've never met Hedinger face-to-face and he is aloof and acts self-important on video calls. Pierre's appearance is always immaculate.

Pierre opens our call. "Your report alleges illegal political activities by our customers. It's essential we include minutes of our call and your report with the agenda for next week's audit committee meeting."

Johanna says, "That's fine. I think my report is self-explanatory and I welcome questions."

Hedinger asks, "Are you saying Louis uncovered a systemic problem involving illegal political activities by our customers?"

"Louis identified two more foreign accounts making illegal political payments. These illegal payments started a year after the account was opened. This is the same pattern identified and reported to your committee by Margot. The shell companies sending and receiving funds all have different customer names to disguise this activity, but similar patterns suggest it's related activity."

Hedinger asks, "Have you detected any issues with our audit committee's role in the oversight of foreign customers and their transactions?"

"No, the bank's oversight systems are working as expected. The bank's account officers monitor all transactions, Pierre's staff reviews the legal status of our customers, my team does periodic audits of customer transactions and we report all suspicious activity to your committee and bank regulators."

"Monsieur Wilson, do you have anything to add?"

"I suspect hostile foreign governments are coordinating these illegal political activities. It's difficult for me to believe the deaths of Margot and Louis are a coincidence. I'm concerned one of these foreign governments may be responsible."

Pierre interjects, "Monsieur Hedinger, the police investigated Margot's unexpected death and Louis's accident. They reported no suspicion of murder. I believe Monsieur Wilson is being melodramatic."

Hedinger says, "Monsieur Wilson, without some evidence, I must agree with Pierre. However, I want the minutes of this call to reflect your concerns."

# # #

Amanda is cheerful when she arrives in Boothbay on Friday night, but her demeanor changes when she sees my sour mood. She asks, "What's wrong?"

"Sorry, my call didn't go well with Johanna, Pierre, and Hedinger this morning. I'm worried about Johanna."

"Why? What happened?"

"She submitted her report describing a series of related transactions being used to influence political activity in Europe. Pierre and Hedinger view her findings as reporting and compliance matters. I suspect hostile foreign governments are coordinating these activities, and one of them might be responsible for the deaths of Margot and Louis. Pierre and Hedinger think I'm being melodramatic. If I'm right, then Johanna is in danger."

"What would be gained by harming Johanna after her report is submitted to the audit committee and bank regulators?"

"You're right, nothing would be gained. I guess I'm disappointed Pierre and Hedinger don't seem to take our concerns seriously."

#   #   #

Saturday is a sunny day and we relax with coffee on the aft deck after breakfast. Amanda says, "I want to enjoy a work-free holiday cruise and plan to drive back tomorrow morning to complete my assignments. The attorneys for the Denver investigation plan to charge Logan, Ashley, and Savannah with insider trading next week."

"They plan to charge Richard with providing inside information to Savannah. Ashley's deposition will determine what future charges they file against Noah and Jacob. The attorneys have these cases under control and they will require minimal time from me while we are away on Paradox."

I add, "I don't expect any activity related to the Paris bank following the audit committee meeting this coming week. Johanna has her audits under control and my client calls are always slower this time of year."

She lifts her coffee cup for a toast. "Let's hope for two weeks of perfect weather and a stress-free holiday."

38

Boothbay Harbor/Aboard Paradox

Moisture from dense fog drips from my jacket on my Monday morning walk to the Red Cup takeout window for my latte. I return to Paradox rather than drink my coffee and read email on my phone at the public landing.

The remainder of my day is spent reviewing client matters and scheduling calls to finish projects before we start our vacation this coming weekend.

#   #   #

Tuesday's virtual audit committee meeting is at two o'clock in Paris, so I log-in from Paradox at eight o'clock in the morning.

As Chair, Sebastian Hedinger opens the audit committee meeting. "We provided each of you with a secure copy of Johanna's report over the weekend. She will discuss her findings and answer questions in a few minutes. I have also asked Monsieur Wilson to join us for this discussion. You may wish to ask him questions when Johanna finishes her report. Johanna, please begin."

Johanna speaks, "Thank you. I believe my report covers all the important details related to our investigation and we are taking appropriate actions to terminate these two customer relationships. We have submitted our report to Interpol and Tracfin, the regulatory authority for investigating money laundering in France."

"I think it's important to brief the committee on the background of our investigation. We believe Margot initiated these investigations before her death. She included the name of both customers in her handwritten notes. We suspect that's why Louis investigated. The handwritten notes from Margot and Louis were in an envelope his wife gave me a week ago. Louis's notes provided the roadmap for our investigation. I will now ask Monsieur Wilson to address the committee before we take questions."

"Thank you. My remarks are pure speculation, but I am concerned about a connection between the deaths of Margot and Louis. Both died shortly after they started investigating these matters. I have no proof their deaths are related to these investigations, but both died under mysterious circumstances. I have suggested both Pierre and Johanna take extra safety precautions. I believe the committee needs to be aware of my concerns. Questions?"

A committee member asks, "I thought Pierre's staff screened all new foreign accounts to confirm they are legitimate organizations. What went wrong?"

Pierre answers, "This is embarrassing. Bank policy requires my staff to verify the authenticity of each customer before we open these foreign accounts. These customers were not flagged as suspicious."

I add, "Pierre, in your defense, the pattern of

transactions would not have been apparent until a year after the accounts were opened. All the original wire transfers were legitimate transactions. These illegal payments were mixed in with legitimate transactions after the accounts were well established. Each transaction is a unique amount to resemble payment for legitimate products or services. These were sophisticated operations."

Pierre says, "Thank you for clarifying."

Johanna adds, "My team is working to identify similar account relationships. I suspect we will uncover more money laundering schemes and I may have recommendations for changes in legal and audit routines."

#   #   #

Amanda calls Wednesday afternoon with an update on the Denver investigation. "Our legal team is proceeding as planned, and they filed all charges on Monday. A high-powered litigation lawyer from a major New York firm is representing Richard, and our lawyers received a call this morning."

"Richard's lawyer said his client will cooperate with our investigation. He assured our lawyers his client has not engaged in any insider trading, nor has he knowingly provided inside information to any third party. Richard wants to cut a deal."

"What do you think?"

"Richard has been caught with 'his pants down', his firm placed him on sabbatical and his wife can't be happy with this publicity. We don't expect to find any evidence he purchased any of these stocks."

"However, Savannah's bank account includes an image of Richard's check for ten-thousand dollars. She opened her brokerage account the same day. Richard funded her brokerage account and traded illegal stock tips for sex. It's no deal for Richard."

"What about Noah and Jacob?"

"Ashley's their problem, she doesn't think insider trading is a big deal – says everybody does it. Her attorney is attempting to portray Ashley and Logan as innocent victims with no legal knowledge. Loyalty doesn't appear to be one of Ashley's attributes. We expect her attorney will try to cut a deal for reduced charges for providing evidence against Noah and Jacob."

#   #   #

Amanda is cheerful Thursday night, "I plan to arrive tomorrow in time for dinner. Everything at my office is under control. How about you?"

"My most important project tomorrow is provisioning at Hannaford's for our voyage."

"Be careful, no more accidents!"

39

Penobscot Bay/ Aboard Paradox

Amanda arrives Friday in time for me to treat her to dinner across the harbor at Coastal Prime. She touches my hand after we are seated, "Nice idea, this view from their outside dining deck is spectacular, it's one of my favorite restaurants. I'm impressed the hostess takes our temperatures when we arrive. This place feels really safe."

I reply, "It's been a busy summer and I want the start of our two-week vacation to be special. It's great to have Paradox in Maine and it's time we take her on an extended cruise."

Amanda says, "I've enjoyed our overnights and the dinghy rides through the harbor – I'm happy anytime we're together."

The waitress arrives with a bottle of Sauvignon Blanc and Amanda says, "My turn to propose a toast – to a vacation without conference calls."

I laugh, "Nice thought, but not likely."

She grins, "Our attorneys have the Denver cases under control. No reason we shouldn't have a quiet holiday together."

"My toast is to nice weather, calm seas, and a wonderful holiday together."

Amanda leans over and gives me a kiss that embarrasses the people at the nearest socially-distanced table.

#   #   #

Kim tosses Amanda our dock lines and we depart Boothbay late Saturday morning for our forty-mile voyage to Rockland.

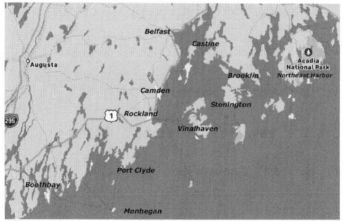
Downeast Maine

Amanda says, "Thanks for arranging our two o'clock tickets to the Farnsworth Museum tomorrow. Everything is by appointment this year due to Covid restrictions, so the museum won't be crowded. I always appreciate their exhibits of Wyeth paintings. What a talented family."

I add, "Rockland offers a choice of restaurants with outdoor seating. We can give you another break from the galley."

Tuesday morning, we cruise the short distance up Penobscot Bay to Camden for two nights. We take the dinghy from our floating dock across the harbor and stroll along the waterfront up to Megunticook Falls Park.

Amanda takes a photo with her phone and I say, "It's tragic to see Camden's schooner fleet still covered in plastic from winter storage. They are usually bustling with crew and visitors eager for a cruise on Penobscot Bay. Covid safety protocols prevent them from sailing with passengers this summer. Our view of these classic schooners in this beautiful harbor offers a sad contrast to our summer cruise."

Camden's Schooner Fleet

Our goal is to support local waterfront restaurants with safe outdoor seating in every town we visit. Wednesday evening, we take our dinghy to the town dock and enjoy a lobster dinner on a deck overlooking the harbor.

Thursday morning, we head twenty miles across the Bay to the historic village of Castine. This historic village was founded in 1796 and, at various times, was occupied by the French, Dutch, and

English. We anchor across the harbor in Smith Cove and launch our dinghy to visit the town.

Castine is home to the Maine Maritime Academy, a public college dedicated to nautical education. The college has scheduled in-person classes starting next week and we encounter a few students in crisp new uniforms as we walk neighborhood streets admiring the community's commitment to preserving its history.

We buy shrimp and crab rolls from the walk-up seafood shack on the town dock and enjoy our view of the Academy's training vessels from a nearby picnic table.

Training Vessels at Maine Maritime Academy

Saturday, we start our forty-mile voyage to Northeast Harbor on Mount Desert Island, home of Acadia National Park. Our voyage takes us down Eggemoggin Reach, by the classic sailing yachts moored in Center Harbor, and east toward Acadia and Northeast Harbor.

40

September - Northeast Harbor

We round Bass Harbor Light, weave our way through an afternoon sailboat race and enter Northeast Harbor's well protected anchorage.

Bass Harbor Light

We celebrate our arrival with a glass of Pinot Grigio and enjoy Amanda's shrimp and pasta dinner Saturday night on the aft deck.

Amanda's excited, "These small coastal towns and harbors are charming. First thing tomorrow, let's go up to the local bakery and buy blueberry muffins and lattes. I'm looking forward to renting bikes and exploring the local trails. Acadia is always more beautiful than I remember. The mountains in Acadia National Park provide such a unique setting around this harbor."

I laugh, "Slow down, we have all week. Here's to a work-free vacation."

#   #   #

Sunday afternoon, I check my email after we return from walking a nearby Acadia trail. I'm reluctant to open an email from Marie.

Steve,

I finally got the courage to sort through the box of documents the bank sent my mother from Margot's apartment. Margot enjoyed writing letters and saved notes, letters, and cards she received from friends and family. Many fond memories surfaced as I sorted through the box.

Margot was grateful for the advice you provided, and she saved dozens of emails and memos from you. I've separated those into a separate box I intend to mail to you. I also discovered an envelope placed inside one of your mystery novels with 'Steve?' written on the outside. I've attached photos of the documents with this email.

The documents have January dates and her notes suggest she planned to discuss them with you – I hope it's not too late.

Marie

Amanda says, "You look troubled."

"Marie sent me an email with copies of Pierre's January bank statement and a wire transfer ticket."

"Why is she sending those to you?"

"They were in an envelope with some of Margot's handwritten notes. Marie thinks Margot intended to discuss them with me back in January."

"Margot circled three transactions on Pierre's bank statement. She circled a deposit from an incoming wire on January 15th for fifty-thousand euros and the entry on January 16th when the incoming amount was reversed. She circled a third incoming wire for thirty-thousand euros on January 20th. Her only note on the bank statement is my name, followed by a question mark. Each entry contains a transaction number for reference."

"The second document is a copy of the January 15th incoming wire from the bank in Lausanne. The funds were wired from The Saint-Prix Family Trust to Pierre's savings account. This ticket shows these funds were forwarded from an account at a bank in Cyprus."

"What does this mean? Why did Margot want to discuss this with you?"

"I need to call Johanna tomorrow."

"Do you want me to take a walk?"

"No, I want you to stay and listen."

#   #   #

Monday morning, I call Johanna in Paris. "Good afternoon, I need to ask some sensitive questions about an account."

"I have a page from a bank statement for account number ###-#####-###. What can you tell me about this account?"

"Just a second. Using my laptop from home is slower than the office system. Are you sure that's the correct account number?"

"Yes"

She hesitates, "It's Pierre's personal savings account."

"Does he have a separate employee checking account for his payroll deposits?"

"Yes, we all do."

"Does he have any other accounts with the bank?"

"No, those are his only accounts. Why is this important?"

"Not sure. What's Pierre's relationship with The Saint-Prex Family Trust?"

"His annual financial disclosure says it's a private family trust he inherited after the death of a relative six years ago. He also inherited a villa in Saint-Prex, and it's his work-from-home location today."

"Does his disclosure form describe the trust?"

"Give me a minute. His annual disclosure says the trust earns income from a securities portfolio and both income and principal may be distributed as directed by the beneficiary. Pierre's report says he has full access to the income and assets of the trust. He reports the trust does not own stock in the bank and the value of the trust is disclosed in a range, between five and ten million euros. His form includes the address for the villa in Saint-Prex."

"OK, that's very helpful. I think it's best we keep this call between us for the time being."

"Sure, can I ask why?"

"Not sure yet, just a hunch."

#   #   #

Amanda's puzzled, "You look worried. What was Margot investigating?"

"I think we are looking at the reason Margot was killed."

"Whoa, that's quite a leap. Why?"

"Look at Margot's note on the top of the wire transfer ticket."

"It's a number, 20-103. Why?"

"Margot established case numbers when she opened new investigations. Louis noticed her case numbers were out of sequence and told me Margot skipped 20-103. We both agreed, Margot doesn't get confused and skip a case number. So, he had the bank's security team search for Case 20-103 on the bank's systems and they concluded it never existed. Margot intended to open Case 20-103 after she returned from New York."

"Are you saying Margot planned to open an investigation into Pierre's accounts?"

"She wrote 20-103 on this wire transfer — what do you think?"

41

Northeast Harbor/Aboard Paradox

"I need to clear my head. It's a lovely day, let's walk up to Main Street for a takeout lunch on a picnic table along the sidewalk."

We order seafood salad with fresh fruit and find an empty picnic table.

"Didn't Pierre tell you he was working from his villa in Switzerland? What did he say?"

"It was a phone call. I remember he asked about New York and I told him I was on the boat. He said something about his old family villa with a view over Lake Geneva."

"I need to learn more, and I hesitate to get Johanna involved. If this is a link to Margot's death, then it will put Johanna in danger."

"What choice do you have?"

"I can start by having Sarah research Pierre's background. I need to learn more about the Saint-Prex Family Trust and the family villa. Johanna said the villa is in Saint-Prex."

Amanda hands me her phone. "Look at this."

Saint-Prex - Morges Region Tourisme

The picturesque and medieval village of Saint-Prex is built on a triangular peninsula stretching along Lake Geneva.

I return her phone and say, "Looks like a nice place to work from home. I've been to Switzerland dozens of times on banking business, but never took time to visit the countryside."

#   #   #

Tuesday morning, my cell phone shows an incoming call from 'Van Gogh'.

"Good morning, Sarah. Anything to report?"

"A start, not finished. I confirmed Pierre was born and attended school in Switzerland. He moved to Paris for law school and joined a prestigious law firm. Pierre became a partner, but he was not elected to the firm's management committee. He joined the bank as Chief Legal Counsel ten years ago."

"I find no record of marriage or divorce. He lives alone in a historic apartment building. He's had an excellent credit score for the past six years, but he showed high debt and past due accounts seven years ago. His social profile has risen in recent years and social magazines show him attending the theater and charitable functions with wealthy widows. I suspect Pierre's considered a socially acceptable male companion for public events."

"The Saint-Prex Family Trust was established in The Bahamas six years ago as an Asset Protection Trust. Bahamian public records do not disclose the name of the settlor or the names of any beneficiaries of the trust. Swiss real estate records show a Monsieur Gabriel Rochat purchased the villa at the same time the trust was organized, but he waited thirty days before he transferred ownership of the villa to the trust. It's common for a trust to own property as part of an estate plan."

"The Swiss agent listed for this Bahamian trust is the private bank you mentioned in Lausanne. It appears the bank manages the trust's assets, and distributions are wired to Pierre. I want to learn more about Monsieur Gabriel Rochat."

"Thanks."

Amanda says, "What now?"

"I need to call Johanna."

#   #   #

"Good afternoon. I have a couple of questions."

"Sure."

"Does my confidentiality agreement permit me to

view all of your audit reports?"

"Yes, you know it does."

"OK, Pierre's disclosure reports are part of the executive officer's year-end report to the audit committee. Can you post the last seven years of his disclosure reports on a confidential 'read-only' file for me?"

"Yes, but I want to know why? This makes me very uncomfortable."

I hesitate, "I have reason to believe Margot planned to open Case 20-103 last January to investigate Pierre's trust. I don't know why and don't want to put you in danger. Please be careful."

"Damn, that's frightening. Don't worry, I'm not leaving this apartment."

#   #   #

An hour later, I receive the password to a new 'read-only' account and spend the next two hours reading Pierre's disclosure reports. When I finish, I email Sarah; *Please call me'*.

#   #   #

This evening it's a call from 'Matisse' and Sarah asks, "Good evening, have you learned more?"

I explain, "Margot joined the Paris bank three years ago, and she added a ten-year summary of financial trends to all her executive and board member reports to the audit committee. Pierre inherited the Saint-Prex Family Trust and villa six

183

years ago. These summaries don't include detailed footnotes, but Pierre's reports confirm he was in debt before receipt of this trust. Pierre reported the trust was established by a relative, Gabriel Rochat, who died in Saint-Prex. All executive officers are required to list significant sources of income, and Pierre reports twenty-three distributions totaling half-a-million euros from the trust to his personal savings account."

"Thanks, I'm still searching for information about Monsieur Gabriel Rochat."

#   #   #

My phone rings during breakfast on Wednesday, showing a call from 'Cezanne'. "Good morning, more news?"

"Monsieur Gabriel Rochat is an interesting man. Rochat is the most common family name in canton Vaud, the location of Saint-Prex. Several men with the name Rochat died between the date the trust was formed and the date it was inherited by Pierre. One brief obituary lists the address of the villa as the man's home."

"The obituary reads; *Monsieur Gabriel Rochat of Saint-Prex passed away on July 17, 2014. He worked for a bank in Geneva for many years and is survived by a cousin who works for a bank in Paris.*"

"The obituary lists the address of the villa, and I've searched public records and credit reports for more information. Gabriel Rochat had a driver's license, voter registration, and two credit cards. Property records indicate he borrowed money from a bank in Basel when he purchased the villa. This mortgage was paid in full when he transferred ownership to the trust."

"His common family name makes finding more information difficult. I'm trying to locate his birth, employment, and burial information. Searching for a Rochat in Saint-Prex is like searching for a Smith in New York."

#   #   #

At noon, I receive a call from Johanna. "Steve, I just had a call from Pierre. He told me the bank's cybersecurity system alerts legal if anyone attempts to access executive officer accounts. Pierre was very cordial and asked why I was checking his bank statements. He is happy to provide any information I request and answer any questions. I told him Margot had a note in one of her files about a wire transfer sent to him in error and I was confirming the matter was resolved."

"Pierre said he remembers talking with Margot about a wire transfer before she went to New York. The bank notified him of a new deposit he wasn't expecting, and when he checked, it was a wire transfer sent to his savings account in error. He immediately returned the funds. He thought the matter was resolved."

"I thanked him and said this will resolve the matter."

I ask, "Did you know about this cybersecurity alert being sent to legal?"

"No, and I'm surprised such a system doesn't alert

both legal and audit. This was news to me."

"OK, this is disturbing. Please don't pursue the matter any further."

# # #

Amanda asks, "What's wrong?"

"Johanna just received a call from Pierre asking why she was checking his accounts. The bank's security department alerts Pierre of any attempts to access executive officer accounts."

"Did you know about this alert system?"

"No, and neither did Johanna. It's also likely Margot and Louis didn't know about this system. Any research they undertook would alert Pierre."

I sigh, "It's time to take a break while I wait for more information from Sarah. Let's take a dinghy ride around the harbor."

42

Northeast Harbor/Aboard Paradox

Thursday morning starts with a call from 'Matisse' and I place my phone on speaker. "Hello, Sarah."

"Steve, I have some disturbing news. Monsieur Gabriel Rochat didn't exist before he moved to Saint-Prex. Gabriel is a ghost, he never existed."

"Humm……….. please explain."

"I became suspicious when the only information about this man started a few months before the Bahamian Trust was established. I was unable to locate birth or employment records. After his death, I found the obituary supposedly submitted by a family member but no autopsy, funeral, cremation, or burial records exist. Last night, I discovered his creator on the dark web."

"Are you are telling me somebody created a fake person to establish a real trust and buy a villa for Pierre?"

"Yes."

"Can we prove that?"

"Yes."

"Thanks, I need to think about our next steps."

Amanda asks, "What's next?"

"I don't know, let's think about it while we walk up to Main Street for a coffee."

#   #   #

As we walk up the hill, I say, "We have two questions; who and why is someone willing to create a fake person to create a real trust and wire over half-a-million euros to Pierre? I think we need to start with their motive."

Amanda replies, "It has to be payment for some greater financial benefit - they expect a financial payback from Pierre."

"That's my first thought, but Pierre isn't a banking officer. He doesn't make investments or approve loans. He can't divert funds to scam investments or approve fake loans."

I pause at the top of the hill. "I might have been too quick to defend him at the audit committee meeting. Pierre's team clears new customer accounts and approves access to the wire transfer system. He is Secretary to the audit committee with knowledge of every audit investigation. If you compromise Pierre, then you have a clear path to launder money."

Amanda adds, "Margot and Louis were both investigating money laundering schemes when they died. Is that the connection?"

"I don't know, this is all pure speculation. We can't

prove a thing. Swiss, Cyprus, and Bahamian bank secrecy laws prevent identifying the source of the money wired from the Cyprus account to Pierre's trust."

Amanda asks, "What about Rochat's mortgage from the bank in Basel? The bank account and mortgage record helped establish this fake identity and money was transferred into a personal account to pay for the villa. What was the source of those funds?"

"Good idea! I'll bet they came from the same account in Cyprus wiring funds to Pierre's trust account. I'll ask Mark if he can make an official inquiry?"

"You should also ask Mark to search our files for your Cyprus account number. I'm curious if it's also connected with one of our money laundering investigations."

43

Northeast Harbor/Aboard Paradox

Mark calls me on Friday. "Sorry, this Cyprus account number is not associated with any of our investigations. You've identified a new suspicious account, so I contacted the bank in Basel. I told them we're investigating money laundering and need to verify this numbered account from Cyprus is the source of funds used to open Rochat's account to purchase the villa."

"I received a return call a few minutes ago. They said they can only release information to FINMA, and I should contact Switzerland's financial markets regulator."

"Another dead end?"

"No, saying 'contact FINMA' is code for the 'account numbers match'."

Amanda asks, "OK, what next?"

"I need to document what I've learned and contact Chairman Richelieu at the bank."

"Amanda, it's noisy if we are underway. Is it OK if we stay at Northeast Harbor and you work from the boat until I resolve this matter?"

"That works for me, don't worry about our return trip."

# # #

"Chairman Richelieu, sorry to intrude on Saturday. My name is Steve Wilson, and I have been consulting with your bank's audit committee and the audit department. I need to discuss some disturbing information with you."

"Yes, Monsieur Wilson, I am aware of your services to our audit committee. Pierre and Sebastian have been very complimentary. What do we need to discuss?"

"I've uncovered some disturbing information. Six years ago, Pierre reported an inheritance from a relative named Gabriel Rochat that included the Saint-Prex Family Trust and a villa in Saint-Prex."

"I'm aware of Pierre's family trust. Pierre discloses this relationship to our board every year."

"I have prepared a brief memo for you describing my concerns. I have evidence Pierre's relative, Gabriel Rochat, never existed. The alleged 'old family' villa was purchased six years ago with funds from a numbered bank account in Cyprus. The trust was established in The Bahamas to disguise its true ownership, and we have a copy of a recent wire transfer of funds from the account in Cyprus into the trust. This account in Cyprus is the source of funds deposited into Pierre's so-called family trust. To be fair, Pierre may have a satisfactory explanation for everything. I have not discussed my concerns with Pierre."

A long pause, "Pierre's relative never existed?"

"That's correct, Gabriel Rochat didn't exist. The villa was purchased when the Bahamian trust was established. It's not an old family estate."

"This is very disturbing information. These are serious allegations. How do you suggest we proceed?"

"I will email my memo to you. I think the next step is for me to discuss it with Pierre and ask him to authorize the bank to review all transactions related to the trust account and the purchase of the villa. He may have a satisfactory explanation."

Another long pause, "Please send me your memo. I'll get back to you."

#   #   #

Sunday morning, I receive a call from the Chairman. "Monsieur Wilson, I have read your memo and shared it with Sebastian. Pierre reports to me and Covid travel restrictions are flexible enough for me to travel to Switzerland. Talking to Pierre is my job and I have arranged for our jet to take me to Geneva. I have arranged a private meeting with Pierre at his villa for ten-thirty tomorrow morning."

#   #   #

My cell phone wakes us Labor Day morning. I hear the beep of a message and my phone starts ringing again. I don't reach it in time to answer, but see the time is six o'clock.

My phone rings as I swipe to check my message and 'Chairman Richelieu' flashes on the screen.

"Monsieur Wilson, I know it's early in the states, but I have sad news. Pierre committed suicide. He didn't answer when I arrived at his villa this morning. I found an envelope with my name taped to the entry door. The note inside said, 'Please come in, I'm in my study'. I found Pierre on the floor of his study, called emergency services, and called the bank's independent counsel in Paris."

"I've been answering questions for the past hour. The police say Pierre died from a single gunshot to his head and they found a suicide note next to his body. Our Paris attorney told me to take photos of his study and the notes. I will text them to you and Sebastian. We can talk tomorrow after I return to Paris."

Amanda yawns, "Who was that?"

"Chairman Richelieu. Pierre committed suicide and Richelieu is texting me a photo of Pierre's suicide note."

Chairman Richelieu,

Please forgive me, I could not face you.

I have no excuse for my actions. I permitted myself to be compromised and accepted money to overlook accounts involved in international money laundering. None of my staff nor members of the audit team were aware of or participated in my activities.

Pierre

"I need to call Johanna."

#   #   #

Amanda brews the coffee while I call Johanna and share the news of Pierre's suicide.

Johanna asks, "Do you think Pierre's responsible for Margot's laptop? He was at her apartment and he reported it missing."

I reply, "Pierre was alerted by the security system that Margot was looking at his accounts. He had access to the bank's audit files and knew she hadn't opened a case file. If he assumed any incriminating evidence was on her laptop, then he could have taken it before anyone reviewed its contents. Damn, I never suspected Pierre."

#   #   #

Amanda says, "I sent a text to Mark. Is there anything more we can do today?"

"No, we can return to Boothbay as we planned. I need to wait on more news from Switzerland. Sorry, this case ruined our plans for a work-free holiday and your vacation is over tomorrow."

She smiles, "Let's enjoy our return voyage, we can get underway after breakfast."

Amanda skillfully pilots the boat as we depart Northeast Harbor mid-morning for our five-hour voyage back to Boothbay Harbor. She is grinning as she dodges the colorful lobster buoys after we pass Bass Harbor Light.

44

Boothbay Harbor/Aboard Paradox

We arrive at Boothbay Marina mid-afternoon and share an early dinner on the aft deck. We take a leisurely walk along the waterfront before going to Amanda's SUV.

I kiss her goodbye, "Sorry. I'm disappointed my Paris investigation interrupted the last week of your vacation."

"Don't worry, it could have just as easily been one of my cases. It's the nature of our jobs."

She gives me a kiss and I watch her drive away. I walk alone to the public landing to view the sunset.

\#   \#   \#

I receive a mid-morning call from Chairman Richelieu on Tuesday. "Saint-Prex's police have ruled Pierre's death a suicide and asked me about releasing his body to his relatives. Pierre's parents are deceased, and he has no siblings or children. We are searching his bank files for a will, and his body is being held at a Saint-Prex mortuary. The police have concluded their investigation and we have access to the villa. This is uncharted territory for me. How do you suggest we proceed?"

"First, I suggest you arrange for private security to guard the villa to ensure nothing is removed. Second, ask your Paris law firm to recommend a Swiss law firm with no relationships to the bank to serve as independent counsel. Third, have this Swiss firm arrange for Johanna and one of her staff to search the villa for all bank records and all records related to our investigation. You want to preserve all phones, computers, and records in Pierre's possession. The Swiss law firm can provide guidance on your ability to remove records recovered at the villa."

"Sebastian has offered to help, what should I tell him?"

"It's essential that he not be involved. The audit committee needs to keep at arm's length and remain in a position to provide an independent assessment of your actions and our investigation. Pierre's death is not the end of this matter. We need to determine why he was compromised and who was making these payments."

Richelieu responds, "I understand. This is a troublesome affair and an embarrassment to our bank."

"Do you have a copy of Pierre's medical report?"

"No, I can ask for one. I overheard the doctor tell the police officers Pierre's time of death was Sunday evening and he died by one gunshot to the right temple. There were powder burns on his skin and the pistol was on the floor next to him. I received a call this morning confirming Pierre's fingerprints were on the pistol and his death was ruled a suicide."

# # #

A few minutes later, I receive a call from Sebastian Hedinger. "Good morning, Monsieur Wilson. I want to thank you for your insightful investigation. I notified the audit committee of Pierre's suicide this morning and we are all in shock. His suicide note didn't explain why he engaged in this illicit financial activity. Do you have a theory?"

"Yes, some person or organization compromised Pierre to cover-up their money laundering activity. Pierre was in a unique position to approve new foreign accounts and grant wire transfer privileges. Pierre was the bank's first line of defense against money laundering."

"Do you think he approved schemes we have yet to uncover?"

"Yes, someone paid Pierre half-a-million euros over the past six years. I expect Johanna to uncover more money laundering schemes."

"You told the committee you were concerned Louis's and Margot's deaths were connected to an investigation. Do you think Pierre was involved?"

"I'm still investigating how Pierre's death might be connected to Margot and Louis. Sorry, my investigation will not be completed in time for next week's audit committee meeting."

"Thank you, the audit committee appreciates your tenacity. Chairman Richelieu said you completed your investigation of Pierre while on holiday. Is that correct?"

"Yes, we were cruising on my boat and visiting Acadia National Park. Our vacation is over and I have returned to Boothbay Harbor."

#   #   #

My next call is to Johanna. "Good morning, I talked to Chairman Richelieu a short while ago and recommended you search the villa for all bank related equipment and documents. I'm curious if you find Margot's laptop."

She interrupts, "He's already called me and I am making arrangements."

"Excellent. I also recommended the bank hire a private security firm to guard the villa. I will talk to him again after our call to make certain you and your staff also receive protection while traveling and working in Switzerland."

"Why? Are you still concerned about our safety?"

"I don't believe Pierre committed suicide with a gunshot to his right temple."

"I'm confused, why not?"

"Pierre was left-handed. Why would he hold the gun in his right hand?"

45

Boothbay Harbor/Aboard Paradox

Wednesday afternoon, I help Kim cast off the lines of a departing yacht. Labor Day weekend is the unofficial end of the summer boating season in Maine and visiting boats are returning to their home ports.

I say, "I'll be back in an hour, I'm low on provisions and need to pick up a few items at Hannaford's."

Kim replies, "Be careful, it took a month to get your bike repaired after your accident."

"Don't worry, I plan to walk my bike down the hill today."

#   #   #

I wait for the light at the bottom of the hill and push my bike into the crosswalk toward Hannaford's. The driver of a car departing the store startles me with a blast of her horn. I hear a screech of tires as another car runs the stoplight with me in the crosswalk. I jump back, my bike is sent flying across the street and I stand stunned with trembling hands at the edge of the street.

\#   \#   \#

"Kim, I need a ride back to the marina."

"What happened?"

"Some stupid driver ran the stoplight at the bottom of the hill and demolished my bike."

"Are you OK?"

"Yes, I'm fine, just stunned. I was walking my bike across the street when a woman leaving Hannaford's blasted her horn. I jumped back, but a car running the stoplight hit the front of my bike, jerked it out of my hands, and sent it flying across the street. It was a close call."

"I'll be right there."

\#   \#   \#

I wait to call Amanda until I return to Paradox. "I had a close call on the way to Hannaford's. I'm fine, but a car coming down the hill ran the light and demolished my bike."

"What did the driver say?"

"Nothing, she kept driving out of town."

"Please don't tell me it was a brunette wearing a fedora."

"I didn't get a look, but a witness said the woman was a blonde with long hair wearing sunglasses and facemask. She was not wearing a hat."

\#   \#   \#

Amanda returns Friday night, and we walk across the footbridge to Coastal Prime for dinner. Amanda appears melancholy, and I ask, "You're not your usual cheerful self, what's wrong?"

"Sorry, the end of summer is always a little bit of a letdown. We only have a few weekends remaining before you ship Paradox back to Florida."

## 46

Boothbay Harbor/Aboard Paradox

Johanna calls Saturday morning, "My assistant and I finished searching the villa for bank equipment and documents. Pierre was meticulous, and it surprised us to find file drawers in the study open and several folders in disarray on his desk."

"We located his bank laptop and cell phone, but not the personal laptop I've seen in his office. We discovered a small wall safe in the master bedroom behind a painting. The safe was unlocked and empty. We found no documents relating to the trust or any of Pierre's bank accounts. Someone else searched his villa before we arrived."

"We also searched the videos on the villa's motion-activated security system for forty-eight hours before Pierre's death. The last videos show Pierre going out for an hour and returning with a bag of groceries Sunday evening. There is no video of Chairman Richelieu arriving Monday morning."

"We have organized all bank equipment and documents for storage at the villa until the attorneys receive permission for us to ship them to our offices in Paris. We've entered photos of each document into the case file. I have provided 'read-only' access for you."

"Chairman Richelieu arranged for a guard from the private security firm to drive us back to Paris. We plan to leave in about an hour and we can't wait to get out of this place. Searching Pierre's villa was disturbing. We could see his blood on the floor in the study."

I reply, "Thank you, I'm relieved the Chairman arranged the guard to drive you back to Paris."

"We will submit a fraud report to FINMA and request access to the trust account after we return to Paris. I asked the attorney to request deleted videos from the security system."

#   #   #

Amanda says, "Thanks for keeping your phone on speaker. Are you surprised she didn't find any records relating to the trust?"

"No, it confirms my suspicions. Pierre didn't commit suicide, and the killer must have forced him to open the safe. Someone wanted all evidence of a connection removed."

47

Boothbay Harbor/Aboard Paradox

Amanda's spirits improve over the weekend and, on Saturday, we enjoy a dinghy excursion to Hodgdon Cove and walk the trails of Oak Point Farm. We relax Sunday with afternoon lattes on a picnic table at the public landing. The boat feels empty when she returns to Portland Sunday night.

#   #   #

Wednesday morning, I receive an update from Johanna. "Swiss authorities don't want negative publicity and can be very cooperative when bank fraud is involved. They granted me access to the trust account's records in Lausanne this morning."

"My analysis didn't take long, and I emailed you a summary with an exhibit. The Saint-Prex Family Trust was opened by Gabriel Rochat with a wire transfer for fifty-thousand euros from a numbered account in Cyprus. An incoming wire transfer from Cyprus preceded all withdrawals by Pierre to his savings account. Pierre also transferred half-a-million euros to a numbered account at a bank branch in Saint-Prex. His total payments from Cyprus exceed one-million euros."

"Trust assets remained at fifty-thousand euros, the

bank's minimum balance for trust administration at the bank in Lausanne. Pierre fabricated its value in his financial disclosure to disguise the deposits to his savings account as dividends. We have a clear pattern of periodic payoffs."

Flow of Funds - Saint-Prex Family Trust			
	Numbered Account - Bank in Cyprus		
	v		v
	v		v
Bank in Basil		Bank in Lausanne	
	v		v
	v		v
Purchase Villa	> > > > > Saint-Prex Family Trust		
		v	v
		v	v
	Bank in Saint-Prex		Bank in Paris
		v	v
		v	v
	Pierre's Secret Account		Pierre's Savings Account

I reply, "Your analysis provides a great summary of dates and amounts wired into the trust. Pierre received twenty-three payments over the past six years, totaling over one-million euros. Individual amounts vary from forty to sixty thousand euros. These had to be significant relationships to justify such large payments."

Johanna continues, "The January wire transfer for fifty-thousand euros Margot discovered was forwarded the same day. Pierre must have panicked when he saw the wire included the incoming account number from Cyprus and returned the funds to Lausanne immediately, claiming the bank sent it in error."

"This gives me the information required to file fraud and money laundering reports with Tracfin in France, FINMA in Switzerland, and Interpol. Chairman Richelieu asked me to send a copy of my report to each member of the bank's audit committee."

"We're also examining Pierre's bank laptop, email, and phone records. Nothing new, everything on the laptop is in our central file, the bank system keeps all email and phone records. We've discovered no suspicious communications."

She continues, "The dates of the payments into his trust account must represent a payoff for each new money laundering account he approved at the bank. My team is investigating all new accounts Pierre approved near those dates. I suspect his record of payments is our roadmap to each new money laundering scheme."

#   #   #

I call Amanda to share the news. "Pierre was a busy man, he received over one-million euros in payoffs over the past six years. He had lavish taste and transferred half-a-million euros to his savings account in Paris to cover his expenses. His savings account has less than five-thousand euros today. He needed the money and had to pay French income tax on these transfers."

"I suspect he didn't trust his benefactor and always transferred excess money in the trust account to a numbered account in Saint-Prex. Johanna just discovered this new account."

Amanda asks, "How did he spend all that money?"

I reply, "The Maître d'hôtel greeted Pierre by his first name and the server treated him like a regular guest. I was surprised when Pierre said a very expensive wine was a favorite. I suspect his appetite for elegant meals, rare wine, custom-tailored suits, luxury automobiles, and social status exceeded his bank salary. That's why he was in debt and susceptible to bribery six years ago."

#   #   #

I receive another update from Johanna on Thursday. "Our Swiss attorney said gaining access to the villa's security system's records was more difficult than the trust account. They report Pierre turned off the security system from inside the villa two hours before his death."

"Humm….. Pierre expected a visitor who didn't want to be seen on camera. How did they communicate? Did Pierre use a burner phone?"

#   #   #

Johanna sends me an email on Thursday:

We're investigating three new suspicious accounts and find Pierre approved two methods to launder money.

The Offshore Trading Company, the investigation the FBI named the Paris Connection, used fake commercial transactions to disguise political activities as payment for equipment and shipping equipment. Offshore used this method to fund illegal political contributions, create fake social media accounts, and disguise payments for political advertising in the United States.

These new accounts utilize a legitimate investment trust organized in France to launder money sent from The Bahamas. The beneficial owner of each French Trust is a Bahamian Trust, so the true owner is disguised. We've discovered investments made throughout Europe by two trusts and the other trust purchased real estate in Florida.

I reply to Johanna's email:

Very clever, nothing suspicious about investments made by a legitimate French Investment Trust.

#   #   #

Amanda calls me Friday afternoon. "I want to give you an update before driving to Boothbay. Our attorneys have concluded their settlement agreements with Logan and Savannah. Both will plead guilty and have agreed to cooperate and testify. They will pay a fine and not face jail time."

"However, Ashley is being stubborn, she says everybody does it and it's unfair to pick on her. Our attorneys are offering her the same deal if she agrees to testify against Noah and Jacob to avoid a large fine and time in jail."

"I promise to arrive in a cheery mood tonight, sorry I was melancholy last week. I want to enjoy our last weekends on Paradox before you ship her back to Florida."

48

Boothbay Harbor/Aboard Paradox

Amanda departs Monday morning with a tear in her eye. "The season's almost over and it's been wonderful having Paradox in Maine. We are very fortunate."

I give her a hug and soft kiss, "Thanks to you, it was your suggestion we bring the boat to Maine."

#   #   #

I call Johanna after my Monday morning walk. "These schemes are sophisticated, but it's disconcerting Margot didn't uncover them earlier. Am I missing something?"

"I had the same feeling and reviewed her audits and the committee's audit policy statement over the weekend. The policy requires audit to notify legal when customer audits are scheduled to avoid triggering unintended litigation. The policy also excludes audits of closed accounts. As a result, bank policy gave Pierre time to warn account owners when an audit was scheduled and the money laundering accounts could be closed."

"In January, Margot wrote a memo to Pierre and the audit committee recommending routine audits of closed accounts. She intended to add her memo to the agenda for the February meeting."

I ask, "Did Louis discuss her memo at the meeting?"

"Louis's notes say Pierre told him Hedinger considers policy changes in December. It was not added to the committee's February agenda."

I respond, "Very clever."

"Not clever enough. Our search for accounts related to Pierre's payment dates shows Margot previously identified three of his money laundering accounts using Limited Liability Companies organized in European Countries to purchase real estate. She sent suspicious activity reports to Interpol and Tracfin after the accounts were closed."

I ask, "She acted before Pierre could block the audits?"

"The accounts were closed after she started and, I suspect, Margot was curious and completed the audits. Pierre couldn't suppress her investigation when she uncovered fraud. Margot cited these investigations as evidence supporting her request for routine audits of closed accounts."

I say, "So, to date, you've identified nine money laundering accounts related to Pierre. Margot's Paris Connection investigation, three accounts previously investigated by Margot, two accounts identified by Louis, and the three new accounts your team's uncovered. Did Pierre know the reason for Margot's New York trip?"

"Margot's notes say she visited with Pierre about her investigation the week before her trip to New York."

I continue, "Pierre had knowledge and access to her apartment. He could have removed her laptop, but you didn't find it in the villa. Have the French lawyers obtained a search warrant for his Paris apartment?"

"Not yet, the lawyers say tomorrow."

I continue, "Pierre was the contact with the police. Please follow-up with them to confirm what they told him about Margot's laptop and the woman in the fedora who departed the service entrance."

#   #   #

Johanna calls me the next morning. "We searched Pierre's Paris apartment earlier today. We found file drawers open and papers in disarray. We didn't find laptops belonging to either Pierre or Margot. We're examining the documents we found, but I believe everything important had been removed. I've asked our lawyers to request images from the security cameras at Pierre's building."

"Margot's building only retains security videos for six-months. It's too late to get copies of activity prior to Margot's arrival."

"My call with the police officer in charge of investigating Margot's death was enlightening. He confirmed they didn't suspect a crime and said they didn't review the security videos. Pierre never reported the missing laptop nor asked about the woman who departed that morning. Pierre fabricated those conversations with the police."

I reply, "Interesting. I asked Louis, not Pierre, to request the security videos. Pierre said the police investigated and the matter was closed. I suspect Pierre was surprised when I asked him about the woman in the fedora leaving the building."

#   #   #

I ponder the news from Johanna and call Amanda. "I'm convinced all three deaths are connected to these money laundering schemes. The list of payments to the trust suggests Pierre authorized over twenty customer accounts to launder money through the Paris bank."

Amanda says, "Even if you're right, would one of those customers murder three people and attempt to silence you. What is so important?"

"I suspect someone had Margot and Louis killed to protect Pierre. They had to have Pierre killed to protect themselves."

49

Belfast, Maine/Aboard Paradox

I call Amanda Thursday night, "How do you want to spend our last weekend? Our summer boating season is coming to an end, and the truck arrives next week to take Paradox back to Florida."

"Let's stay at the marina and take the dinghy across the harbor to Prime Coastal for dinner on their deck Saturday. I want to enjoy our last weekend in Boothbay before you take Paradox to Front Street Shipyard."

#   #   #

Amanda hides her emotions when we walk to her SUV early Monday morning. She gives me a soft kiss and says, "Love you. Let me know when you arrive in Belfast."

#   #   #

I call Amanda Tuesday afternoon after arriving at the shipyard. "The seas were calm and the sky was cloudless. It was a spectacular way to end our summer. I need to finish getting the boat ready for her truck ride back to Florida. I've made arrangements for Paradox to go to Stuart rather than Palm Beach. It's better to be in a county with lower Covid cases. Sunset Bay Marina is ready for her and I hope we can travel to warmer weather again this winter."

# # #

Amanda calls the next day, "Get everything done?"

"Just a few last-minute details. It's the end of the season and the docks are busy. Front Street is getting three large yachts ready to sail south."

"When do you plan to come back to Portland?"

"I've picked up my rental car and will depart as soon as Paradox is on the truck. I should arrive tomorrow in time for dinner."

I pause, "Any news today?"

"We are wrapping up our insider trading case. Ashley accepted our deal and both Noah and Jacob have agreed to plead guilty, pay a significant fine, and consent to be barred from employment in the securities business. I learned Jacob's wife has filed for divorce."

"Richard's attorney is trying to negotiate less jail time for him if he pleads guilty and pays a substantial fine. I think we will agree to a deal rather than go to trial. He will be disbarred and his wife has filed for divorce."

"Our attorneys will present these settlements to the judge in October, and the case should be closed by the end of the month."

# # #

We move Paradox to Front Street's travel lift late morning. The boatyard crew uses the pressure cleaner to remove barnacles from her hull and they move her to a nearby truck trailer. I'm amazed at how large Paradox appears when she's out of the water and that a truck can move her on the highways from Maine to Florida.

It's silly, but I wave goodbye and walk alone to a waterfront restaurant for lunch. Summer aboard Paradox has been a welcome respite from Covid restrictions in Portland. The restaurants are now open, but I have no interest in eating inside and the weather will soon turn too cold to eat outside. Our future is uncertain, but I have no current plans to go back to New York or Florida.

50

October - Portland, Maine

Friday is my first day back in Portland, and we return to our previous routine. Amanda brews the morning coffee, toasts bagels, picks up her leather backpack, and departs by seven o'clock. I take my morning walk and settle at the desk in Amanda's alcove.

I'm blocked by bank secrecy regulations from identifying the owner of the Cyprus account wiring money into Pierre's trust account. Humm…..Maybe I will have better success from the other direction and I email Sarah.

I get a call from 'Monet' an hour later.

"Sarah, I think it's time to go shopping. Can you search the dark web for Swiss banking contacts? I want to identify potential contacts to help me launder money through Switzerland. I'm looking for someone who networks with multiple clients."

"Sure, that's easy, but it will be a long list. I was going to call you today. I may have a lead on the person who killed Margot, Louis, and Pierre."

She continues, "I've been monitoring the dark web

for women assassins for hire. A woman using the name Ruslana fits your profile. She is reported to be about the age of the woman in your photo and she has a reputation for preferring to stage her hits as accidents, natural death, or suicide. She has declined several recent proposals saying she is on assignment."

"Any confirmed photos, fingerprints, or DNA?"

"No, her identity is a mystery. Her online name reflects her reputation for successful assassinations. Ruslana is a woman's name meaning 'Lion' and is of Russian origin. You will learn more if you have Mark send Interpol your photo and ask if it's Ruslana."

#   #   #

I email Mark and attach the security camera photo.

This woman departed the building's service door an hour after Margot arrived. Her overnight bag is large enough to hold Margot's laptop. It's possible this woman calls herself Ruslana. Can you inquire if Interpol has any information that might be helpful?

#   #   #

I'm fixing a sandwich for lunch when I hear the bell at the apartment's door. I'm not expecting visitors and check the peephole. I see a woman with short red hair, wearing green medical scrubs, holding her medical facemask with an Amazon box.

I keep the door closed. "Hello. Can I help you?"

"Hi. I'm Sally from 203 on the second floor. I just

217

got home from work and found this at my door. It's for Amanda in 303, it was left outside the wrong apartment."

She raises the Amazon box higher so I can see the label through the peephole.

"Just a minute."

51

I unlock the apartment door and she gives me the Amazon box. I say "thank you", confirm the address label, and face a small pistol with a silencer when I look up.

"Keep your mouth shut and step inside."

"Whatever you say."

The woman closes the door behind her, looks around the apartment, and directs me toward the desk in the alcove. The desk faces the window and she stands behind me.

"Sit down with your hands on the desk. Is that your laptop?"

"Yes. Do you want me to stop the music?"

"Turn up the sound. That's good. What's your password?"

I hesitate and she says, "Speak up!".

"FL5047PW"

"Type slow so I can watch you open it."

I click the keys with trembling fingers.

"Write your password on the pad."

"Go to the master file for Pierre's case. What's the password for those files?"

"FL2175AX"

"Open the file and put your password on the pad."

"Any other passwords to open Pierre's files?"

"No."

"Open a few at random to confirm you're telling me the truth."

I click and open a few file folders.

"I have a few questions before I depart with your laptop."

I feel beads of sweat on my forehead and turn my head to look her in the eye. "Sure, may I call you Ruslana?"

Her eyes penetrate mine - - - if looks could kill.

I continue, "We've been looking for you – but I'd rather meet you under better circumstances. You have an excellent reputation for suicides and convenient accidents. I'm surprised you missed me going down the hill."

She laughs, "Nice try, but that wasn't me. I was behind the stupid driver who ran the light and caused your bike accident."

"What about your other attempt?"

"Not me. The marinas and waterfront streets are too public for a clean escape."

"Why target me?"

"Getting too close to the truth about Pierre."

"Pierre's dead, who wants me out of the picture?"

"Shut up. I'm asking the questions. You will go to your grave without his name."

I see Amanda slip into the alcove archway behind Ruslana's right shoulder. She's holding her Glock with both hands and it's aimed at Ruslana.

Ruslana asks, "Who else knows my name?"

Amanda calmly says, "I do. Drop your weapon and raise your hands."

Ruslana replies, "Yes ma'am." She slowly appears to comply but snaps a sudden turn. Both pistols discharge and Ruslana falls to the floor. Amanda steps forward and kicks her pistol away.

"Call 911. We need an ambulance and the police."

It takes me two attempts to dial 911 with my trembling fingers.

My legs feel like spaghetti as I stand and hold the side of the desk for support.

Amanda keeps her pistol aimed at Ruslana and says, "Roll on your side so I can see your wound."

She hands me a pair of handcuffs. "Put these on

her ankles and bring me the medical kit in the bathroom. We need to stop this bleeding. We don't want her to die."

Ruslana spits, "Bitch, you won't be able to hold me!"

I return with the medical kit and carefully pass a large gauze pad to Ruslana for her to hold on her bloody shoulder.

The ambulance crew arrives followed by two police officers. Amanda shows her FBI identification. Ruslana's cuffed to the stretcher and Amanda accompanies her to the emergency room.

#   #   #

I'm answering questions from a police detective when Mark calls, "Amanda reported she discharged her weapon and injured a suspect. How are you?"

"My hands are still shaking. I'm damn glad Amanda showed up."

Mark says, "Interpol sent me a classified profile on Ruslana. She is reported to be a skilled assassin for hire. Your curiosity about Ruslana's relationship to Margot's death concerned me. I called Amanda and told her to return home."

"What information can you share about Ruslana?"

"Interpol's report said there are no fingerprints, DNA, or confirmed photos of the woman known as Ruslana. She has a reputation for disguising her kills as accidents, suicide, or natural causes. Her reported age, height, and weight fit your photo and the deaths of Margot, Louis, and Pierre all match her style of execution."

"I'm being questioned by a police detective. What should I tell him?"

"Tell him you are working with the FBI and hand him your phone. I'll explain the situation."

The detective finishes his call with Mark and says, "I understand the FBI will handle this investigation. We'll secure the crime scene and be on our way."

He places the standard yellow tape across the door to the apartment and takes photos. He also places tape across the entry to the alcove and instructs me not to interfere with any potential evidence.

#   #   #

Amanda returns to the apartment two hours later. She stoops under the yellow tape on the door and I give her a long affectionate embrace the instant she stands. She asks, "Are you OK?"

"My hands are still shaking and I'm too nervous to sit for more than a few minutes. I'm damn glad you returned home when you did."

"Mark called and said he didn't want you alone."

"How did you know she was inside?"

"The door was unlocked. I heard voices when I cracked it open and decided it was best to be quiet. The music helped cover the sound of my entry."

223

"That's ironic. She told me to turn the music louder, probably to cover the sound from her pistol."

I pause, "Damn. She looked believable in her scrubs, acted like she was being helpful, and the box was addressed to you. I made a stupid mistake."

Amanda says, "Relax, I don't know all my neighbors and I would have opened the door."

She continues, "An agent from Boston will arrive in an hour to interview us and examine the scene. Mark wants an independent report prepared."

#   #   #

"Whew, I'm glad that's over. That guy acted like you were being reckless to fire your weapon. I'm impressed you remained so calm."

"Just doing his job. I would have acted the same. Ruslana won't accuse me of unnecessary force, but we follow the same procedure every time."

"Why did he take the package?"

"He'll check for explosives or poison."

I exhale, "Damn. I think we both need a Scotch. Did you learn anything from Ruslana?"

"No, she's uncooperative and refuses to answer any questions. We are rotating agents with her overnight and I will return to the hospital tomorrow morning. My shot hit an artery in her right shoulder, but she's not badly injured. We can move her to a more secure area tomorrow. You hungry? I'm starving and ready to fix dinner."

#   #   #

My phone rings and I'm surprised to see 'Renoir' calling me.

"That was a close call. Ruslana doesn't make mistakes. Are you OK?"

"Yes, I'm fine. I won't ask how you know."

"Simple, my system monitors Amanda's address and emergency dispatches aren't encrypted."

#   #   #

Amanda's phone wakes us at four o'clock; "Hello?"

"What! Are you hurt? I'll be there in twenty minutes!"

"Ruslana's gone! Damn, she had backup."

"What happened?"

Amanda grabs jeans and a sweater. "The agent on duty said a doctor stopped by to check on her condition and he remembers nothing after turning to sit. He woke up with a nasty gash on his head and Ruslana was gone."

52

Portland, Maine

It's four o'clock in the morning, Amanda's at the hospital, and I'm restless. I brew coffee, review email, shuffle papers on my desk, and check the weather report. It's late Saturday morning in Paris, so I place a call to **Chairman** Richelieu.

"Bonjour, sorry to disturb you on a Saturday, but I believe Pierre's killer paid me a visit yesterday."

"Monsieur Wilson, what happened?"

"A woman confronted me with a pistol yesterday. I believe she killed Pierre."

"She killed Pierre?"

"Yes. I'm certain Pierre was killed. I believe she intended to steal my laptop and kill me. She demanded access to my files about Pierre and our money laundering investigation. Johanna has access to all the same information, and her safety is my primary concern today. It's essential she has 24-hour protection until we resolve this matter."

"Monsieur Wilson, the safety of my employees is my highest priority. The private security company we hired is already providing protection for

Johanna. Please tell me more about yesterday. Were you harmed?"

"No, I was rescued and the woman was apprehended. It's a long story, but she escaped. We believe she's an assassin for hire that uses the name Ruslana. I'm working with the FBI and will keep you posted as our investigation unfolds."

An hour later, I receive a call from Sebastian Hedinger. "Monsieur Wilson, I understand you had a close call yesterday. What happened?"

"I prefer we don't discuss the investigation until it's ready for presentation to your committee. We are at a very sensitive stage and I called Chairman Richelieu this morning to make certain Johanna has 24-hour protection."

"I'm Chair of the audit committee, and the bank has experienced a tragic betrayal by Pierre. Shouldn't I be fully engaged in this investigation?"

"It's best you let bank management, financial regulators, and government investigators conduct independent investigations. You and the audit committee are responsible for oversight of management's response. The audit committee can't provide independent oversight if it's involved in management's investigation."

"When do you expect to have a report?"

"We will share the results of our money laundering investigation with Chairman Richelieu, the audit committee, Interpol, and financial regulators when the investigation is complete. I'm confident we will identify the people behind this scheme. Chairman

Richelieu will be kept informed of significant progress and the audit committee will receive our comprehensive report."

He sighs, "Thank you, and please be careful. Your life is more important than this investigation. Chairman Richelieu and I don't want another casualty."

#   #   #

I can't go back to sleep, so I get a fresh cup of coffee and open my laptop to review our investigation. What is so important? What am I missing?

Amanda returns at eight o'clock. "Glad you made coffee, the stuff at the hospital is horrible."

"Anything you can tell me?"

"Let's call Mark after I get a bowl of cereal – I'm starving."

#   #   #

Amanda dials Mark's number, places her phone on speaker, and says, "Good morning, thanks for responding to my text messages from the hospital. Mike needed stitches but is otherwise unharmed. Ruslana's escape was a smooth operation in the middle of the night. The floor nurse was diverted by a false request at the other end of the hall and didn't see anything. The night guard told me he saw a doctor with a woman in a raincoat walk across the parking lot to a car and drive away."

"When I checked the security cameras, I could see

a man wearing scrubs and a facemask push a wheelchair up the hallway toward Ruslana's room. A few minutes later he exits with Ruslana in the wheelchair. The camera at a side door shows him helping Ruslana put on a blue raincoat and they walk into the parking lot. He was careful and avoided the cameras in the parking lot. We have no useful description of the car or the man who helped Ruslana."

Amanda sighs, "This is embarrassing, I never suspected she worked with a partner."

Mark interjects, "I approved the hospital plan; we are both responsible. The good news is, for the first time, we have Ruslana's photo, fingerprints, and DNA. It's likely we will determine her family name and nationality. She won't be able to hide in plain sight any longer."

I ask, "Do you think she will be apprehended?"

Mark replies, "I doubt it. She's escaped detection for over a decade. I suspect she's accumulated enough money to disappear with a new identity. Amanda took her photo and Interpol's new face recognition software is her biggest challenge. Plastic surgery will be on her agenda."

Amanda says, "Ruslana needed to be restrained when we took her fingerprints. She was really pissed when I removed her short red wig and took photos with my phone. 'Bitch' is my new nickname. I think her short blonde hair is her natural color but she was wearing stage makeup."

Amanda asks me, "How did she know you were at my apartment?"

"She said she watched a careless driver cause my bike accident. She was already watching us in Boothbay and followed me to Portland."

Amanda grins, "That's creepy. I suspect she is a master of disguise and we probably walked past her on the sidewalk in Boothbay."

I look at Amanda, "You were in the doorway when she said I would never know 'his' name."

Amanda says, "That's right. She referred to her employer as a man, not an organization."

Mark asks, "Any idea who he is?"

I answer, "No idea."

Mark says, "Let's consider some alternatives:"

"First, you've been focusing on hostile foreign governments. Recent examples suggest they target individuals when those people are a threat to their state's leadership. You are not a threat to any nation's leadership; therefore, I doubt 'he' represents a foreign government."

Second, criminal organizations are more likely to use physical intimidation and assassination as an enforcement tool. 'He' does not represent a criminal organization forcing you to commit a crime.

"Third, 'he' knows your whereabouts."

I reply, "Let's start by identifying men associated with the Paris Connection who know my whereabouts."

Amanda adds, "It's easy to track Paradox. The boat transmits its position over the Automatic Identification System and all you need is a mobile phone app for the AIS network."

Mark says, "We need to start somewhere. What about the bank in Paris?"

I sigh, "It's a short list: Chairman Richelieu, Sebastian Hedinger, Pierre, and Johanna. Pierre monitored the schemes, he knew we were on the boat, and he could share our relationship and location with anyone. I have no doubt, Pierre was the source. Ruslana was following me in Boothbay before I returned to Portland."

Amanda asks, "How would she travel between Europe and Maine with Covid travel restrictions?"

Mark answers, "US citizens are permitted to return to our country. I have no doubt she could fly with fake passports and avoid Covid travel restrictions. Covid quarantine compliance relies on the honor system."

I'm exasperated, "The woman hired to kill me escaped and we don't know who hired her. I won't feel safe until we do. Damn, I'd like some fresh air, but I'm afraid to go outside today."

53

Portland, Maine

After our call with Mark, I pour a fresh cup of coffee and slouch on the living room sofa. I'm deep in thought when Amanda joins me, "Any ideas?"

I say, "Margot's Paris Connection and Louis's accounts channeled money to political activities. I got sidetracked when I thought we were looking for connections to a hostile government."

"However, Johanna's discoveries are all typical money laundering programs used to clean money and hide ownership of assets. The amounts, location, and type of assets purchased all vary. Individuals and criminal organizations want to hide ownership of assets. These accounts represent more than one person or organization."

Amanda says, "Could the man we're looking for be a financial architect structuring money laundering schemes for numerous clients? Pierre could identify this architect and was eliminated."

"Good observation, I've been working in circles. My initial focus on the political aspects was a distraction. Pierre was the common link to all these accounts, but he was not the financial architect."

I sigh, "It's evening in Paris. I'll review the files again tonight and we can call Johanna tomorrow morning."

#   #   #

"Bonjour Johanna, sorry to call on a Sunday. Pierre was a busy man over the past six years and your team is doing an excellent job. Your idea to search for new foreign accounts opened at the time Pierre received a payoff is proving to be an effective short-cut to locating suspicious accounts. I've added your three accounts to my list."

Money Laundering Accounts Identified

Margot: 4 Investigations
- *'Paris Connection': Political activity in USA*
- *LLCs to purchase stocks & real estate [3]*

Louis: 2 Investigations
- *Fund political activity in Europe*

Johanna: 3 New Investigations
- *French trusts: stocks & real estate*

I continue, "My investigation started with Margot's trip to New York to discuss the Paris Connection with the FBI. This account was being used to fund illegal political contributions and post fake news on social media accounts."

"You discovered three other schemes uncovered by Margot. These accounts were using Limited Liability Companies to purchase securities and real estate."

"Louis identified two commercial accounts using Limited Liability Companies to direct funds to illegal political contributions and social media advertising in Europe."

"You've identified three French Investment Trusts organized to buy securities and real estate."

"I don't see a pattern yet, do you?"

"No, the only common link we see is Pierre. Everything else is a jumble."

I spend Sunday afternoon examining the suspicious real estate transactions Johanna discovered. I construct a diagram of banks and real estate brokers involved in each transaction. Once again, no consistent relationships.

#   #   #

Amanda has a new desk delivered Sunday afternoon and rearranges the bedroom to give her a private space to work. Late-afternoon, she announces, "I need to go to the office for an hour to collect some files. Please, don't open the apartment door while I'm away."

She returns home an hour later. "Mark called while I was at the office. He explained how Ruslana was able to enter the apartment building. A stolen car was in the parking garage next door and the security cameras show a woman in blue coveralls leave the garage carrying a box. Ten minutes later, this same woman follows a plumber through the service entrance into my apartment building. Blue coveralls were found in the trash can in the stairwell between the second and third floors."

I grimace, "So that's how she got past security. I

suspect she did something similar in Paris."

Amanda asks, "You make any progress today?"

"I've researched every real estate transaction Johanna's uncovered and see no common links to our architect. Each French Trust used local real estate agents and arranged cash transactions. I see no common connections."

Amanda looks at my diagram. "This is a mess. This couldn't be more confusing if it was done on purpose."

I smile, "That's correct. These transactions all disguise any common connection. Our financial architect used Pierre to authorize international wire transfer privileges for multiple clients. Foreign governments are associated with the political contributions and social media campaigns. I suspect we have a wide variety of individuals and organizations laundering money into securities and real estate. The only common connection we can identify is Pierre."

Amanda says, "It's time to take a break and you are grilling steaks on the balcony for dinner. Too bad we couldn't keep Ruslana's package. She has a strange sense of humor. The agent said she had two bottles of expensive French Bordeaux in the Amazon box for me. It's being stored as evidence."

54

Portland, Maine

After breakfast, Amanda and I take a morning walk along the Portland waterfront. I say, "Thanks for playing bodyguard. We need to solve this case so you can return to your office. It's your apartment, I'll switch desk locations if you prefer to work in your alcove."

"Not necessary. My new desk in the bedroom fits nicely and it's working fine. With Ruslana on the loose, we can't send you out for a walk when I need privacy."

Amanda finds me in a sour mood at lunchtime and brightens my spirits with a kiss.

"Thanks, it's been a frustrating morning. I'm stumped. I can't trace the money wired into these French trust accounts back to its source. Pierre is the only common link between all the money laundering accounts. I can't identify how Pierre communicated with the architect. He must have used a burner phone."

"Johanna's team is doing an excellent job of identifying suspicious activity, closing accounts, and filing reports with bank regulators. My objective is to identify the person who arranged for

Ruslana to kill Margot and Louis. Every time I start down a path, it's a dead end."

Amanda gives me a hug, "It's time for lunch and you're fixing clam chowder for us today."

#   #   #

Amanda's on her phone with the bedroom door closed all Monday afternoon. I'm still at the alcove desk when she emerges at five o'clock.

"My bedroom office worked fine today. How was your afternoon?"

"Another day puzzling over these Paris bank account connections. I've concluded I don't know how to investigate."

She sits in the chair next to the desk. "Can we talk about it?"

"Sure, I need your insight."

I say, "Follow my logic. First, our financial architect has to be someone with knowledge of banking and investments."

"Second, he has to be someone who would benefit financially by facilitating money laundering."

"Third, it's someone that knew Pierre was seriously in debt six years ago."

"Fourth, it's someone who could have frequent private communication with Pierre, probably using a burner phone."

"Fifth, it's someone with knowledge of my whereabouts after Pierre was dead."

Amanda replies, "I agree with your first two assumptions. Anyone with financial connections could check Pierre's credit reports and criminal organizations all use burner phones to communicate. Pierre told Ruslana you were in Boothbay and she followed you to Portland. Your assumptions are valid, but they don't help limit your search."

"I know, that's the problem."

55

Portland, Maine

Tuesday morning, Amanda takes her backpack and plays bodyguard on my morning walk before we start our workday. She emerges mid-morning to refresh her coffee and finds me deep in thought at my desk.

She asks, "How's it going?"

"I think the answer finally hit me while I was looking at Pierre's telephone log this morning. Let me show you."

Amanda pulls a chair next to mine and looks over my shoulder at my laptop. "I don't see any suspicious names. You've confirmed everyone on this list is a legitimate relationship."

"Who made the last incoming call to Pierre?"

"Sebastian Hedinger."

"Pierre turned off his security system five minutes after Sebastian's call."

Amanda sits looking at Pierre's phone log. "If Sebastian's the architect then Pierre didn't need a burner phone. They had an official relationship and

---

239

talked frequently. He sure fits the profile you outlined. It's hard to believe Hedinger could be the architect. How do you plan to proceed?"

"That's my dilemma. You have any suggestions?"

"Your suspicions are all circumstantial. Is there any way to prove a connection?"

"I want to know how this started. Johanna's team started with the date for the most recent payment into the trust. I want to look at the first transaction. Chairman Richelieu hired Pierre ten years ago and the bank's legal department always had responsibility for screening new foreign accounts."

"Sebastian Hedinger joined the board ten years ago and became Chairman of the audit committee eight years ago. Pierre inherited the villa and fake trust six years ago. Margot was Chief Auditor for three years before her death. I want to know what happened six years ago. I need to email Johanna."

Johanna,

Your team is doing an outstanding job of working down Pierre's list of payments. However, I have a request. I want to learn how this started six years ago. Please scan for new foreign commercial accounts and French trust accounts opened three months before the first payment to Pierre's trust. I want to identify the first money laundering account Pierre approved for international wire transfers.

Steve

56

Portland, Maine

Johanna's reply is on my laptop when I check email Wednesday morning.

There were six commercial and four trust accounts opened and approved for wire transfers. One account for the Offshore Investment Trust [France] was in limbo for six weeks before receiving approval from Pierre for international wire transfers. It was approved the same day as the first deposit into Pierre's savings account.

I text Johanna and ask for the Offshore Investment Trust [France] customer profile. To my surprise, she adds it to my 'read-only' file in thirty minutes.

I'm busy reviewing Offshore's profile when Amanda walks from her bedroom office to the kitchen to refresh her coffee. She asks, "Any progress?"

"Maybe. Johanna sent me information about an account for Offshore Investment Trust [France]. The customer profile says the trust was organized by a client of Hedinger's firm and he introduced the trust to the Paris bank. Pierre's staff rejected wire transfer privileges for the trust's account and it remained inactive. Six weeks later, Pierre authorized wire transfer privileges. The account was closed a month after Margot joined the bank."

"I've sent a text to Johanna asking her for details on each of the wire transfers to and from this account."

#   #   #

Two hours later, I receive a text from Johanna:

Offshore Investment Trust [France] was opened and funded by Offshore Investment Trust [Bahamas], a client of Hedinger's investment firm. All additional deposits were wired directly from The Bahamas. I have attached the list. The outgoing wires were all sent to New York banks for the purchase of real estate.

It's after ten o'clock at night in Paris, so I text Johanna:

Please check the nine money laundering accounts you've identified to date for any other incoming wires originating at Hedinger's investment firm – thank you.

Johanna sends me a text Friday morning:

No other incoming wires originated from Hedinger's firm. Please call me!

#   #   #

Johanna asks, "Why are you interested in incoming wires from Hedinger's clients?"

"It might be a coincidence. The first payment to Pierre's trust occurred the day he granted wire transfer privileges to the Offshore Investment

Trust [France]. I wanted to see if there was a pattern. What does the customer file say about Pierre's approval?"

"The customer profile doesn't explain why Pierre authorized wire transfer privileges. Would you like me to undertake more research?"

"No, please load the complete file for the Offshore Investment Trust on the system and I'll take it from here. I suspect you should keep this to yourself."

#   #   #

My next two hours are spent cross-checking dates with phone calls, wires from Cyprus to the Saint-Prex Trust, deposits to Pierre's savings account, and Pierre's authorization of wire transfer privileges for each of the nine accounts suspected of money laundering.

I send an email to Sarah asking her if she can locate any information about Offshore Investment Trust [Bahamas] and Offshore Investment Trust [France].

Thursday morning, I receive an email from Sarah.

Someone is using these trusts to disguise their ownership of real estate in New York. Offshore [Bahamas] was established seven years ago and all ownership information is private. The trust's assets are managed by Hedinger's investment firm in Switzerland.

Offshore [France] was established thirty days after the Bahamian trust was organized. Today, Offshore

[France] is listed as the owner of twelve LLCs organized in New York and each LLC owns an office building. The LLCs all have a tax ID, bank accounts, and operate as legitimate tax-paying businesses. Dividends can be paid to the trust in France and then paid to the account in Switzerland.

This appears to be a typical 'layering' operation to 'clean' the source of 'dirty' money used to purchase real estate. There may well be other accounts used to 'wash' the money before it arrives in The Bahamas.

57

Portland, Maine

I spend Friday afternoon drafting a memo describing the sequence of events related to Pierre's approval of wire transfers for the Offshore Investment Trust [France]. My next step is to analyze the relationships between wire transfers, phone records, and Pierre's approvals for each of the money laundering accounts.

At dinner, Amanda asks, "Any progress you want to discuss?"

"Not yet, I want to complete my research, finish my memo, and get your opinion tomorrow. I'm in the mood for a Humphrey Bogart movie tonight."

#   #   #

We take our regular morning walk on Saturday and I sequester myself in the alcove to work on my analysis all morning.

"Ready for lunch? I plan to make ham and cheese sandwiches today."

"Good timing, I'm ready to review my memo with you after lunch."

#   #   #

We sit on the sofa in the living room after lunch and I open my laptop. "I believe Sebastian Hedinger is our architect, but I don't want to accuse him of bank fraud without proof."

"How are you going to prove Hedinger's the architect?"

"I don't know. Everything I have is circumstantial, but I've documented a six-year history of potential evidence. My memo outlines questions Hedinger needs to address. I plan to send my questions with exhibits to Chairman Richelieu Monday morning. But first, I want to review my timeline and supporting documents with you."

Timeline for Offshore Investment Trust Approval:

- 8 yrs ago: Hedinger elected Chair of audit
- 6 yrs ago: Hedinger introduces Offshore
- Legal staff rejects wire transfer privileges
- Rochat Family Villa purchased
- Saint-Prex Family Trust established
- First payment into Pierre's trust account
- Hedinger phone call to Pierre
- Pierre transfers payment into savings account
- Pierre approves wire transfer privileges
- Pierre calls Hedinger
- Funds used to purchase real estate
- 3 yrs ago: Margot selected as Chief Auditor
- Offshore account closed [1 month later]

"To date, we've identified nine other suspicious accounts Pierre approved for international wire transfers. I've identified the dates of payments into the trust and phone calls between Pierre and

Hedinger before each approval. Each of these accounts engaged in money laundering. My exhibit shows the payments and their phone conversations all occur the same day Pierre granted wire transfer privileges."

Timeline [same day] for 9 other accounts:

- Payment into trust account
- Call from Hedinger to Pierre
- Pierre transfers payment to saving account
- Pierre approves wire transfer privileges
- Pierre calls Hedinger

Amanda says, "You've been very thorough, but each point is circumstantial. Pierre and Hedinger have a working relationship and he can deny calling Pierre to authorize wire transfer privileges for these accounts."

"You don't know the owner of the account in Cyprus that wired the payments to the Saint-Prex Family Trust. Hedinger can claim his last call to Pierre was business, and Pierre must have used a burner phone for his fraudulent activities. You haven't proved Hedinger is the architect."

I'm discouraged. "I have to start somewhere. We never have proof, only suspicions, when we start an investigation. I feel an obligation to discuss my suspicions with Chairman Richelieu. If he agrees, then I need to call Hedinger."

I pause, "I want to have a witness on my calls. I want you to listen to our conversation. OK?"

"Sure, but I will need to ask Mark."

58

Portland, Maine

Amanda brews coffee and we go to the alcove at five o'clock Monday morning to call Richelieu.

"Bonjour Chairman Richelieu, I have prepared a memo we need to discuss today. When you have an hour, I will email my memo with exhibits so we can discuss it together."

"It must be important, you're up early. I can be available in ten minutes. I will tell my secretary to hold my calls."

# # #

"Monsieur Wilson, you never fail to surprise me. This memo and your questions are very disturbing. Have you discussed any of this with Sebastian?"

"No, I wanted to share it with you first."

"I have known Sebastian for over twenty years. I invited him to join our board when I became Chairman. Both he and his firm are highly regarded in international financial circles. I can't believe he is associated with money laundering."

"As I explained, I feel an obligation to share my

questions with you before discussing them with Monsieur Hedinger."

"These are serious allegations and I prefer you discuss your questions with Sebastian. I'm eager to know what he has to say and hope he has satisfactory answers."

"I understand, I'll call him."

#   #   #

"Monsieur Hedinger, I have prepared a memo with questions we need to address today. When you have an hour, I will email my memo with exhibits so we can discuss it together."

"Is this related to Pierre?"

"Yes."

"I will hold my calls, please email it now."

"Let me know when it arrives."

"Got it. [long silence] What the hell is this?"

"It's a draft memo. I want to resolve these questions with you before it's submitted to the audit committee."

In a loud voice. "Are you accusing me, the Chair of the audit committee, of some impropriety?"

"I want to give you an opportunity to provide answers to my questions."

"I don't even recall introducing this customer to

the bank – this was six years ago. Chairman Richelieu expects all board members to introduce new customers."

"My memo allows you to explain the sequence of events related to Pierre's actions, the organization of the trust, his fictitious inheritance, and his subsequent approval of wire transfer privileges."

He shouts, "This has nothing to do with me – this is preposterous! I have a meeting in a few minutes. I'm warning you, do not distribute your memo. My attorney will contact you."

I look at Amanda, "Well, that didn't go well. I need to call Chairman Richelieu."

#   #   #

"I regret to say my conversation with Sebastian went badly. He got angry and hung up, saying his lawyer will contact me. I expect to receive a call from his attorney and hope to explain the importance of a detailed response."

"My memo is published by my firm, so your bank is not responsible. I sent Sebastian a follow-up email saying I will wait 24-hours to hear from his attorney; otherwise, I am distributing my memo to the audit committee."

Richelieu responds, "These are serious questions. Is there anything I should do?"

"I suggest you contact the bank's outside legal counsel, share my memo, and ask for advice."

#   #   #

The next morning, I see an email from a Swiss law firm sent at four o'clock, my time, asking me to call the attorney for Sebastian Hedinger.

"Bonjour, this is Steve Wilson."

"Thank you for calling. I read the most interesting memo prepared by your firm yesterday. What do you intend to do?"

"My email to Monsieur Hedinger says, in the absence of a response from him, I intend to submit it to the bank's audit committee tomorrow. If he wishes to provide answers to my questions, then I will wait for another 48-hours."

"That's not much time to respond. Your questions suggest my client was involved with Pierre's money laundering schemes."

"My questions have straightforward answers if he is not involved."

#   #   #

The following day, I'm emailed a letter from the law firm representing Hedinger with a revised copy of my memo attached. It has been amended to include the following response to each question:

Our client denies any knowledge of wrongdoing or involvement in these matters.

The letter from the law firm says Hedinger will hold me liable if I distribute any copies.

An hour later, I email a copy of the law firm's letter and the amended memo to Chairman Richelieu and

Johanna. I request both documents be distributed for discussion at the next audit committee meeting.

I also email Sarah:

Please review the attached memo and exhibits. Does this information match any potential money laundering schemes you have discovered on the dark web?

We exchange messages an hour later:

I've identified contacts on the dark web offering to use investment trusts at French banks to launder money, but the only way to identify the source of the offer is to respond. I'm reluctant to expose myself.

I reply:

Don't risk exposing yourself. Just monitor any related activity. This may not be the connection, but Ruslana's visit proves I'm getting close.

# # #

The next 48-hours are silent, the only communication is a brief call from Johanna on Friday. "Wow, you sure kicked over the bucket this time. Chairman Richelieu asked me to distribute my monthly report, the lawyer's letter, and your amended memo to the audit committee for a virtual meeting next Monday. Monsieur Hedinger is furious and plans to participate with his attorney. Chairman Richelieu wants you to attend Monday's video conference."

59

Portland, Maine

The virtual audit committee meeting convenes at two o'clock in Paris on Monday. I see Chairman Richelieu, Johanna, and the bank's outside counsel wearing facemasks and sitting six feet apart at a conference table. Each member of the committee is visible, and I see Hedinger is accompanied by his attorney.

Chairman Richelieu opens the meeting and invites Hedinger to respond to my memo.

Hedinger's face is flushed. "Monsieur Wilson's memo and his allegations are preposterous. My attorney is distributing my official response to you today, and I will summarize the important points."

"First, as board members, we are all expected to introduce new customers to the bank. I didn't recall introducing the Offshore Investment Trust to the bank and asked my staff to prepare a summary. We opened a substantial investment account for this organization seven years ago, and I introduced them to the bank six years ago. At no time have suspicious transactions been brought to my attention by my firm's audit staff. No concerns were brought to the attention of this committee while this firm was a customer of the bank."

"Second, my attorney reviewed the dates of all my telephone conversations with Pierre and we have provided a complete list for the committee. The few calls highlighted by Wilson's memo represent a small fraction of our calls and the timing he notes are all circumstantial. I never discussed authorizing wire transfer privileges for any customer with Pierre."

"If Monsieur Wilson's allegations of money laundering by Offshore Investment Trust are accurate, then my firm is a victim of this conspiracy, and we will close their account and file a suspicious activity report with FINMA, Switzerland's financial regulator."

"Chairman Richelieu, with your permission, my attorney wishes to address the committee."

"I have advised my client to refrain from further comment and Swiss financial regulations prohibit sharing additional information concerning his firm's client. The allegations in Wilson's memo are false and we will take legal action if it is distributed by Wilson, the bank, or members of this committee."

Chairman Richelieu asks, "Monsieur Wilson, do you wish to add any comments?"

"Thank you, my memo outlines questions related to the bank's investigation of Pierre's involvement in money laundering. My aim is to give Monsieur Hedinger an opportunity to address these questions for your committee. In my opinion, his response does not address each of my questions."

A woman committee member speaks, "Monsieur Chairman, the committee members wish to convene in a private video session."

# # #

My computer screen goes blank and I walk to the kitchen for a glass of water and return to my desk. Thirty minutes later, my computer screen comes back to life.

The woman committee member says, "Our committee has reached a consensus."

"Monsieur Wilson, your memo raises serious questions related to Sebastian's relationship with Pierre's money laundering activity. However, your evidence of possible collusion is circumstantial."

"Sebastian, your presentation today was sincere, but your written response does not address each question and doesn't provide us with evidence you were not associated with Pierre's actions."

"We have a dilemma. We understand Swiss financial regulations prohibit disclosure of customer information, but we are obligated to know the facts. We appreciate your offer to file a suspicious activity report with FINMA. The committee is directing Johanna to join your action and file suspicious activity reports for Offshore Investment Trust and the Saint-Prex Family Trust with FINMA. We believe it's best you recuse yourself from audit committee meetings until we know the results of FINMA's investigations. We expect FINMA to exonerate you, but we feel an obligation to be thorough."

Hedinger erupts, "This is outrageous, I am Chair of this committee and I have no intention of recusing myself!"

The woman is unperturbed, "That's not your decision."

"Bullshit!" Hedinger's video picture goes blank.

Chairman Richelieu sighs, "I accept your decision and you may discuss this matter in a private session of board members tomorrow."

The woman replies, "Thank you. This is a delicate matter and I suggest we limit our private session to board members only, without Monsieur Hedinger or Monsieur Wilson in attendance."

Richelieu says, "Monsieur Wilson, we appreciate your attendance today. I will let you know what the board decides. Johanna, please proceed with your regular report."

My computer screen goes blank.

#   #   #

I tap on Amanda's door, she replies, "Just a minute."

The door opens and she says, "Let's get a fresh cup of coffee. How did it go?"

"Inconclusive. Hedinger's firm and the bank are filing suspicious activity reports with FINMA. The committee directed Hedinger to recuse himself from audit meetings until FINMA concludes its investigation. Hedinger became hostile as you might expect. Richelieu plans to discuss my memo in a private session with board members tomorrow."

\#   \#   \#

Chairman Richelieu calls Tuesday afternoon. "Your memo was discussed in our private session today and it received a mixed reception. However, everyone agrees your questions deserve appropriate answers. The board approved the audit committee's recommendation to file suspicious activity reports with FINMA. I appreciate your efforts to identify the person or organization that compromised Pierre, but I hope you are mistaken and it's not Sebastian."

Johanna calls me on Wednesday. "We filed our report with FINMA this morning. We included your memo as amended by Monsieur Hedinger's attorney. What do you expect to happen next?"

"I have no idea. FINMA is protective of Switzerland's financial reputation and has no obligation to disclose its findings. Any news from Hedinger?"

"Not a word, and he didn't attend the board meeting."

60

Portland, Maine

Thursday morning, I receive an email from Hedinger's attorney.

Monsieur Wilson,

We have attached a copy of our lawsuit alleging you slandered Sebastian Hedinger and his firm.

Please have your attorney contact me so we can resolve this matter and limit the damages you will pay.

Amanda asks, "What will you do?"

"Nothing. It's a bluff expecting me to change or withdraw my memo. Johanna included my memo with her filing to FINMA, and I hope they use it as a roadmap for their investigation."

"What if Hedinger isn't the architect?"

"In that case, he has a right to be angry."

#   #   #

Mark calls us Friday morning, "FINMA contacted me this morning requesting a reference on you and additional information about the Offshore Investment Trust's wire transfers to purchase real estate in New York. We've joined their investigation of these transactions."

I respond, "That's good news. How long do you want Amanda to work from home?"

"You and Johanna aren't safe until we know who hired Ruslana and we solve this case."

I laugh, "Don't worry, Amanda won't let me go outside this apartment without my bodyguard. I'm pleased Chairman Richelieu is providing security for Johanna."

Mark asks, "How's the new arrangement working?"

Amanda answers, "We've established a new daily routine and it's working. I join Steve for his morning walk and close the door to my temporary bedroom office for privacy when we return."

"I can assign another officer to serve as temporary bodyguard if it works better. Steve's a witness and we want him protected until we resolve this case."

Amanda smiles, "Not necessary. We both feel fortunate to be working and sequestered together."

#   #   #

Tuesday morning, my phone rings with a call from 'Gauguin'.

"Good morning Sarah, any news?"

"I did a little research and set my tracking system

to monitor traffic related to Hedinger. His private jet departed this morning and landed in Cyprus. That's all I know."

# # #

Mark calls us Tuesday afternoon. "Interpol reports Hedinger departed Zurich this morning on his private jet for Cyprus and disappeared after he landed. It's not clear how he complied with or bypassed Covid restrictions. Tracfin, the French financial authority, is involved and Interpol has posted an alert for his arrest on suspicion of money laundering."

I'm shocked. "What? Why did he disappear and why is Interpol involved? My memo only presented circumstantial evidence."

Mark says, "Your memo provided a roadmap for FINMA's investigation. FINMA won't share their results, but I suspect they discovered Hedinger owns the account in Cyprus. He probably flew to Cyprus to withdraw cash and disappear."

# # #

Mark calls on Wednesday afternoon, "Hedinger's attorney contacted the FINMA attorney today and said Hedinger's offering to cooperate. His attorney said Pierre was blackmailing Hedinger. He believes Pierre hired Ruslana to kill Margot and Louis. He claims Ruslana killed Pierre to eliminate him as a witness to her crimes."

"How did Pierre compromise Hedinger?"

"The attorney said Pierre identified Offshore

Investment's money laundering scheme and threatened to expose the relationship to Hedinger's firm. The attorney said Hedinger fired the account officer involved but agreed to pay Pierre to avoid embarrassment. Once it started, he couldn't stop paying blackmail."

"That's a unique defense, Pierre's dead and Hedinger told the committee the Offshore account at his firm is still open. Will the Swiss negotiate a deal with him?"

"I don't know. I told FINMA we will proceed with prosecution for money laundering."

#   #   #

Mark calls us Friday during breakfast. "Interpol reports a servant discovered Sebastian Hedinger's body last night at a waterfront villa in Croatia."

"What happened?"

"The local police said it was suicide."

#   #   #

Amanda and I sit speechless at the kitchen table until a call from 'Morisot' breaks our silence.

"I assume you know a servant found Hedinger's body in Croatia and the police say it was suicide."

"Yes, Mark called."

"Hedinger rented the villa under an assumed name and paid cash. The police discovered his Swiss passport in his luggage."

"Can I ask how you know?"

"Sure, my scanning software picked up his name on a local news site. The death of a financial fugitive from Switzerland is a big deal in this small town, and it's posted on their local news sites and social media accounts."

"Amazing, not much remains secret these days."

"Rumors say Ruslana retired after she killed Hedinger to eliminate him as a witness. Her contact site on the dark web has disappeared."

#   #   #

Mark calls us with an update on Monday. "The Swiss closed Hedinger's investment firm this past weekend. They have no plans for a public announcement."

I ask, "Will any of Hedinger's clients engaged in money laundering be arrested or prosecuted?"

Mark sighs, "I suspect his clients are all shell organizations designed to hide true ownership. We've sanctioned individuals at the hostile nation we linked to the Paris Connection. However, their efforts to disrupt our democratic elections won't stop. Worldwide cyberattacks by agents of hostile nations are the new cold war."

He continues, "We have better success with criminal organizations and individuals attempting to hide assets. It's a constant cat-and-mouse game of prosecutions leading to confiscation of assets."

"What about Ruslana?"

"Ruslana is a ghost today, and she will be difficult to apprehend and prosecute. She has been careful, and no solid evidence ever connected her to an assassination. Holding you hostage and firing at Amanda are her only crimes."

"What about the security photo from Paris?"

"Circumstantial, it only places a woman resembling Ruslana at the building. It provides no proof Ruslana was in Margot's apartment."

#   #   #

Tuesday morning, I open a text from Johanna.

The Swiss discovered Margot's bank laptop at Hedinger's villa in Zurich and are returning it to the bank!

#   #   #

The next morning, I receive a call from Chairman Richelieu. "Bonjour Steve, I want to thank you for your persistence in helping us unravel this betrayal by Pierre and Sebastian. We want to add a bonus to your compensation, so I was shocked when Johanna said you volunteered to work without pay. That's absurd, and I wish to pay your normal fee plus a bonus."

"Not necessary, I did this for Margot."

Epilogue

November – Déjà vu

I return to the apartment Wednesday afternoon holding bags of groceries in both hands. Amanda removes my facemask and greets me with a kiss. "How does it feel to go outside without your bodyguard?"

"Weird, I still look over my shoulder and double-check traffic when I cross a street. I sure hope Sarah's right and Ruslana is retired."

"I have a pork roast underway for tonight and you will have leftovers for sandwiches this week. I hope you don't feel deserted during the day, but I'm more productive working at my office."

"Thanks for playing bodyguard. I hope we can establish a more normal work routine, even with Covid safety restrictions. I never thought I would miss walking through airports and boarding a flight. Putting on my facemask is now second nature, but I do miss face-to-face meetings."

Amanda says, "The restaurants are open, but I'm still reluctant to eat inside. Let's take advantage of the few remaining warm days, outdoor heaters have limitations and it will be a long winter."

I give her a hug. "That's fine with me, but the only reason to eat at restaurants is to give you a break from the galley. Our menu is much better at home with your spontaneous creations."

I continue, "The leaves were turning bright red and orange along the roads on my drive back from Belfast. Let's play 'leaf lookers' this coming weekend and drive north to the lakes and mountains for a change of scenery."

She smiles, "That's a wonderful idea. What have you decided about trips to Paradox this winter?"

"I'm reluctant to return to Florida until we see an effective vaccine distributed and new Covid infection rates are under control. Maybe I'm overly cautious, but I feel safer with you in Maine."

Amanda smiles, "And………."

I give her a soft kiss, "I love being together."

About the Author

Charles and his wife, Molly, and their dog, Scupper, enjoy cruising in The Bahamas and along the east coast from Florida to Chesapeake Bay and Maine aboard their Duffy 37, a custom Maine-built lobster boat.

Charles enjoyed a fifty-year career in the banking industry having served as an executive officer and as a board member of several banking institutions. His Paradox Murder Mystery series blend his financial experience with his love of cruising.

Additional information is available at:

www.Paradox-Research.com

Paradox09A@Gmail.com

Appreciation

Molly

Linda, Martha & David

Acknowledgments

Our summer cruises in Maine provide extensive information and insight about the locations described in Paris Connection.

I am very grateful to the following:

Boothbay Harbor Marina
Brooklin Boat Yard
Front Street Shipyard

Photos

Molly Potter Thayer

Shutterstock:
Samot, Rick Neves, Iuliia Gatcko
Daniel Jedzura, jenlo8

Death Trap

A Paradox Murder Mystery
Book One

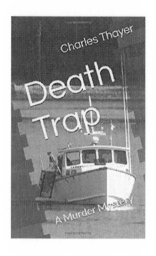

Steve's years of unraveling financial mysteries from the safety of his bank office do not prepare him for the danger he faces in Maine when his curiosity about a dead lobsterman, a deserted lobster boat and three missing photos almost get him killed.

Learn how the story begins as Steve Wilson travels to Maine to unwind, enjoy the coastal scenery and write a murder mystery novel.

Turquoise Deception

A Paradox Murder Mystery
Book Two

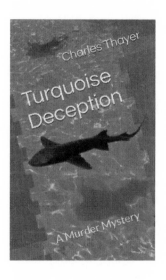

The banker's body is discovered shortly after sunrise in Thunderball Grotto, an underwater cave located in The Bahamas. The banker lied to both his boss and his wife when he told them he was going to Florida to attend a banking conference. Why he deceived them about the conference and died in the turquoise waters of Thunderball is a mystery.

The Bahamian authorities call his death an accidental drowning. The bank suspects an embezzlement when hidden cash is discovered and hires Steve Wilson to investigate.

Deadly Curiosity

A Paradox Murder Mystery
Book Three

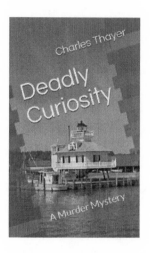

A tragic accident, a cybersecurity intrusion, and a mysterious blonde leads Steve into a complex web of unanswered questions. Join him as he investigates suspicious political contributions and an international money laundering scheme.

Moving his boat from Palm Beach to Chesapeake Bay for the summer places Steve closer to the answers and to dangerous political intrigue.

Synthetic Escape

A Paradox Murder Mystery
Book Four

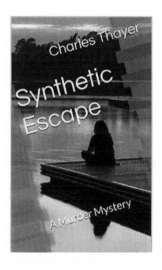

Steve's visit with a classmate at his 40th high school reunion challenges his memory of a tragic death. He discovers old friends are not what they seem and have secrets to hide.

His investigation of a potential fraud intersects with a tangled web of deceit, blackmail, and murder. Will a second-rate movie offer the killer a path to escape the past and retire in luxury?

Books by Charles J Thayer

Fiction

2020 Synthetic Escape, A Murder Mystery

2019 Deadly Curiosity, A Murder Mystery

2019 Turquoise Deception, A Murder Mystery

2018 Death Trap, A Murder Mystery

Non-Fiction

2017 Bank Director Survival Guide

2016 Credit Check
Giving Credit Where Credit Is Due

2010 It Is What It Is
Saving American West Bank

1986 The Bank Director's Handbook
Auburn House: 2nd Edition
Chapter: Asset/Liability Management

1983 Bankers Desk Reference
Warren, Gorham & Lamont
Chapter: Financial Futures Market

1981 The Bank Director's Handbook
Auburn House: 1st Edition
Chapter: Asset/Liability Management

Made in the USA
Middletown, DE
19 May 2023